The Culture of Deceit

"Who watches the watchers?"

by

Rod Hacking

Copyright © 2019 Rod Hacking

All rights reserved.

ISBN: 9781081275891

To Lucy Trevitt

Quis custodiet ipsos custodes?

(Who watches the watchers?)

– *Juvenal*

Previously . . .

In *Emily and the Boss* we learned that Alex Elliot amidst much acrimony resigned as the youngest Bishop in the Church of England after just two years in the job, having previously been Professor of Philosophy at Cambridge. A friend, Oliver Stretton, head of *The Poetry House*, a major publishing company suggests to Alex that for a complete change he might accompany and manage a reading tour across America by one of his poets, Emily Cunningham.

Despite the age difference, each is smitten from the first and soon they are lovers. In Los Angeles she is declared to be his fiancée.

From Seattle they make for Vancouver but having checked in for their flight in their hotel the traffic is so bad they are too late and miss the plane and have to go by bus. Only later do they learn that the plane had crashed with total loss of life including, according to the newspapers and television in Canada and the UK, their own.

Returning to England they find somewhere to live in the Derbyshire Dales and then Emily discovers, to their mutual delight, that she is pregnant and the hospital scan confirms twin girls.

There is much more in the book which is also concerned with smuggling works of art out of Italy and a group of drug pushers totally bamboozled by Emily's friend, Anne-Marie, also known as The Boss.

Chapter One

The Noble Lord, Lord Mehta of Zetland, entered the Members Room and made straight for the bar where he ordered a brandy and dry ginger. At first glance he thought he had the room to himself, but then noticed the head of just one other. He wanted some time with a newspaper and having collected what he was looking for turned towards an empty corner when he saw whose head it was he had spied.

'Alex Elliot,' he said, 'how simply splendid to see you.'

The other rose and shook his hand.

'And you, Jacob.'

'May I join you?'

'I'd be delighted.'

'Before anything else I must tell you that I bought your wife's latest collection and I think it so good I have bought more to give away to those I think will appreciate good poetry. It's remarkable how she has so successfully changed her style.'

'I'll report back and she'll be delighted to hear it. Feedback helps.'

'And what's it like being married to a famous poet, and one called Elliot, though of course she still writes as Cunningham?'

'Because I'm not a poet, to answer I would quickly run out of superlatives.'

'And do you miss your previous distinguished occupations and titles?'

Alex laughed.

'Not in the slightest. But what about you? How is life in the Lords?'

'Mostly I'd rather be at Lord's Cricket Ground. You didn't make it to the Lords, did you?'

'No, I wasn't in post long enough'

'Well, Alex, you were spared a fate worse than death. Politics has become an unpleasant and messy business, and I have known in my lifetime nothing like the present time for being a nation divided and a parliament divided into quite so many factions. If I lived north of the Border I would vote for independence at the first opportunity. It worries me a great deal.'

'Though I imagine it's far worse in the Commons.'

'Definitely, but it spills over inevitably, and I regret to say it has turned formerly good people into liars and perpetrators of discord. There's been unpleasantness before, as when Nye Bevan called Tories vermin, but it's not so long ago that dear old Dennis Skinner was suspended from the House for calling Cameron "Dodgy Dave". Now you would probably have to commit murder during Prime Minister's Questions to share his fate.'

Alex laughed.

'I'm sure you will know what I mean when I tell you that meetings of the Peak District National Park Trustees sometimes resemble a battlefield. At first I tried to stop the warfare, but last time I reached for a book from my bag and began to read. When it was noticed, people quietened down, which was a pity as I had reached a good bit.'

'Was it the Book of Common Prayer?'

'Now that's a good idea. I'll try it next time.'

'But do tell me, do you function as a bishop or priest now, because if my theology is correct you can't be un-bishoped or un-priested?'

'In terms of mediaeval thought that is certainly the case, but to be honest Jacob, that doesn't mean anything to me anymore. I certainly don't think of myself in that way and the last thing I'm likely to find myself doing on Sunday morning is attending or taking a service.'

'You have children now I gather.'

'Twins, a boy and girl and trust me that when you hear the word 'handful' it will never do justice to these two wonderful creatures whom I adore. It's quite funny. When Emily had her scan we were told for certain that it was going to be two girls, and the first one to emerge was a girl as expected, but we all had something of a surprise to discover that the next was most definitely a boy. So much for technology.'

'Oh well you might get your wish when he later declares himself to be a woman. It's all the rage apparently.'

'Yes, it's all rather odd. But today is a very special day, because it's my day off. Most of the time I'm the full-time carer to give time and space to Emily for her writing, but do you know, I am learning so much from them, and I spend a great deal of my time with them laughing. It's also the most exhausting thing I've ever had to deal with in my life, and I know Emily would say the same.'

'You're absolutely right and it reminds me of years ago when mine were at the same age and stage. If it's any consolation, I would say it doesn't last forever, and certainly not until after their 35th birthday, until then it's worry all the way!'

'Thank you Jacob, I shall be in my seventies then, but I'm looking forward to it very much indeed.'

'Actually I wasn't being totally honest. It doesn't stop at 35 at all, it lasts for ever. I was just trying to encourage you. But do tell me, does your childcare allow you any space for doing some writing?'

Alex looked at his watch.

'Very little at the moment but I'm not complaining, but I fear I must leave you and begin the journey home. I've been doing the Renaissance Exhibition at the Royal Academy and if you haven't been yet, do so. It's superb.'

Alex began to prepare himself for leaving.

'Are you going home by train?'

'I can't think that anybody in their right mind would drive down the M1 and into the centre of London, so yes, I shall head towards St Pancras and Emily will meet me, with the twins, at the other end.'

Jacob stood and took Alex's hand.

'I'm so glad you weren't killed in Canada in that awful plane crash which you and your wife missed because you were too late.'

'Better late than late. We both talk about it quite a lot. Anyway it's good to see you Jacob, and if I were you, I would try to spend more time at Lord's than in the Lords.'

To the north of the city of Kingston upon Hull lies Banklyn Prison, a Category A establishment holding up to 800 or so men, all of whom are serving sentences longer than seven years, a high security prison for housing many of the most dangerous criminals, including terrorists. Among them is Theodore Armstrong, normally known as Teddy, who was sentenced to life imprisonment, and not less than 20 years, in 1999 for the abduction, rape and murder of two children in the Lake District. As an inmate he kept his head down, caused no trouble and took advantage of the educational opportunities offered to study for a degree with the Open University in Computing and IT, all of which stood him in good stead as his appearance before the Parole Board drew near. If he was released on licence, he would have to agree to be monitored closely and he was already on the sex register for the remainder of his life, something which caused him no concern whatsoever for in effect it had no meaning at all as most of those on the register with him know only too well.

The process of preparing for a Parole Board was considerable. Although if he won release, he would be expressly forbidden ever to visit the Lake District which pained him for he had missed it every day of the previous 20 years. He was hoping instead that he might be allowed to live in Derbyshire, near the Peak District. Teddy knew that the process would take six months and that at the end of the process the decision of the Board would depend wholly on whether they judged him still to be a significant risk to the public after release. He thought that if it went ahead, he might be at risk from the parents in Cumbria, who maintained that they would find him if he was ever released and exact the appropriate revenge. He regularly received letters from them saying this and he made sure they were handed over to the governor, who assured him that if he was released he would be given a new identity. He thought about freedom every day but he would have to wait. He had jumped through all the psychological hoops and psychiatric hurdles they had insisted on, here and in Wakefield, where he had spent the first ten years of his sentence. Here he was with appalling human beings, especially the Moslem extremists, who, like everyone else, he detested..

Although the staff and especially the screws with whom he came into daily contact knew that he was playing the system in the hope of parole, they detested him for his crimes. As far as they were concerned, locking him up and throwing away the key was too good, and whilst he was relatively safe in a high security prison such as Banklyn, many of them would have wished him to spend even just 24 hours in a less secure institution and would take great delight in how he emerged, especially if he did so in a box.

Anderson Wilson (Andy to his friends), the governor, had

responsibility for those who had done despicable things, and despised Armstrong more than most. He did not believe that the man should ever have parole, and still could not believe that the trial judge had set a tariff of 20 years before parole could be considered. He completely and utterly mistrusted the prisoner and knew only too well, because he had seen it before, that he was playing the "totally reformed" act. Reports which had gone to the Board commenting on his mental state in relation to his crimes showed only too clearly how this horrible man had succeeded in pulling the wool over the eyes of the medics and do-gooders who call themselves psychologists, whom he thought were a bunch of wankers, an opinion widely shared by his staff. Although there was never going to be an occasion on which he would express himself, Andy believed that the return of capital punishment would not only save a lot of money, but would remove from the human race some of those who did not deserve to be in it.

George and Chloe were still fast asleep, and it did sometimes happen that their mid-morning nap extended over the lunch period, allowing Emily and Alex some quiet time together. The post had just arrived and Alex was particularly interested in an official-looking letter from the Cabinet Office but passed it over to his wife to open.

'It's all to do with the Parole Board. It seems that they are appointing suitable people to serve as a liaison between the members of the Board and a particular prison so that when decisions are made about an individual, the link person can offer their advice based on their own observations and conversations. It says it arises from recent controversies about early release. Anyway, they would like to appoint you to be their link person with Banklyn Prison near Hull. Good heavens! I have a feeling that's the place where many of the most serious offenders are housed. What do you make of that?'

'Well, I suppose it was inevitable that at some time my past would catch up with me in terms of having held so-called responsible positions in the Community, so in that sense it doesn't altogether surprise me. I'm obviously seen as one of the great and the good with nothing better to do. But it wouldn't altogether be inappropriate to suggest that the Archbishop of Canterbury has planned this in the hope that I might get locked up and can't get out.'

Emily laughed.

'Does it say what sort of time commitment it would involve? There's no way I would undertake anything that takes me away from you and the twins too much.'

'Here darling, read it for yourself.'

She passed it over to him and inwardly she smiled for she had some time back realised that Alex needed glasses for reading and was too vain to acknowledge it. He could manage still with the computer because he could change the font size but he had noticeably not been reading the newspaper quite as much and he always handed over to her his letters. She was going to have to say something soon.

A baby was crying, almost certainly George, but he would thereby wake up his sister and soon they would be desperate for something to eat, and probably need their nappies changing and their clothes. Ah, she thought, thank goodness for her husband whose day on duty it was. She would go and try to write.

Child-minding, especially double child-minding, meant no time for thinking, reading and certainly not for writing, so Alex threw himself into the task allotted him with gusto. The twins were not yet walking so the three of them would lie down together on the carpet and be silly together which they adored and made them laugh. The former philosopher and diocesan bishop had never been happier and already the memory of those days and responsibilities had begun to fade. It was now rare for a newspaper or television to make contact asking for an interview, he turned down every invitation to write articles for philosophy magazines and journals, something he knew he would never return to, and the church seemed to have forgotten about him completely which suited him, and unquestionably suited them.

Even though the twins were tiny, he did like to read them a story. He knew they could understand nothing but their concentration on the book and the pictures and his words simply amazed him. After their lunch, some of which occasionally flew through the air, he gave them their bottles of Emily's expressed milk. She was talking about weaning them, but was reluctant to give up the breast quite yet. Breast feeding twins requires a lot more skill than doing so for a single child, and whereas Emily fully appreciated why some mothers abandoned the breast, she knew she had been fortunate in finding that it worked for her and the twins.

Alex liked nothing more than a trip into Sheffield with the twins, not least because the rocking motion of the car usually sent them to sleep. They went to the children's section of a bookshop. He was tempted to try his hand at writing a book for children and considered the possibility of "Topsy and Tim Screw Up The Church of England" (though, frankly, they didn't need to bother as it was being done quite successfully without them!). Just thinking about it gave him great pleasure and there was another he had in mind, which would be dedicated to his former philosophy department at Cambridge called "How To Talk Through Your Bottom", which he thought all children would enjoy, as all children, it seemed to him, loved anything to with farts!

Outside the weather was being generous so once home he decided to take the twins for a walk in their double-buggy. There was no doubt that the Peak District was a wonderful place to live.

Not only was there amazing beauty, but it was full of interesting people he was delighted to have got to know. Quite often he had to pinch himself to remind himself that it was real, that not only had he escaped from the prisons of University and Church, but that through the percipience of his friend Oliver he had come to meet and fall headlong in love with and then marry Emily, and as he looked at the two creatures before him, he could see the fruits of that love. No doubt he pinched himself again.

Emily did the bath and Alex did the supper which they could settle down to eat once George and Chloe were asleep, which happened quickly.

'Have you managed to get anything accomplished today, darling?' he asked.

'Nicky emailed me with one or two suggested changes in some of the poems I sent a couple of weeks back. I really do trust her judgement and I feel we're on the same wavelength so when she makes a suggestion I give it full consideration.'

'I suppose that's what an editor is for. And do you make the changes she suggests?'

'Oh no!' She giggled. 'But then again Nicky knows me really well.'

'How often do you speak to her?'

'About once a week mainly to gossip.'

'And dare I ask if she is still together with Claire?'

'Definitely. I'm so happy for her. She is now head of *The Poetry House* and happily settled with a lovely partner, and she reports that Oliver never interferes, though it would be difficult now he lives in Sicily, and is himself a new dad – at his age!'

'I'm so pleased for them all. I shall never forget seeing Lizzie's face at Anne-Marie's wedding when she found herself in that wonderful church that looks more catholic than the catholic and out came a woman priest. Poor Lizzie had never seen anything like it in all her days. Which reminds me is there news from north of the border?'

'Oh I'm sorry, I should have told you. It's most exciting. Anne-Marie's pregnant and Ed has resigned his job with the First Minister and is hoping to train as a psychotherapist. Until then he will work on the farm with Anne-Marie's assistant, Rhona. She's the one you said you fancied when we met her, and if you remember I hit you!'

'That's because you didn't let me finish my sentence. I was trying to say that I fancied her but not as much as you, and now I have to live with the sort of terrible permanent bruising that at my post-mortem will cause the pathologist to be concerned.'

'There's a saying in the North of England: "Tha' sez owt but tha' prayers".

Alex roared with laughter.

'And it's more true than anyone knows.'

'In the meantime have you had any time to think about the letter that came today?'

'An afternoon with the kids doesn't lend itself to serious thought, as I'm sure you know, and perhaps, before I turn it down, it would be sensible to have a conversation with the appropriate person at the Cabinet Office and learn a little more about it. If I were to do it I think I would have to give up my chairmanship of the National Park, which would be a great blessing in itself. The Banklyn job is also paid which I imagine we would both welcome.'

'Well you will have a little more time tomorrow as my mum is coming to look after the children. Quite where she gets her energy from I just don't know.'

'I know what you mean. In so many ways she is such an amazing lady and I bet that when she was younger, she was as pretty as a picture.'

'Oh she was and of course pure white, unlike her brown daughter.'

'You rarely mention it. Do you ever received comments?'

'None at all. Things have changed in this country in a big way and nobody seems to notice or mind.'

'Chloe seems to have inherited it more than George, but I think it makes the pair of you look wonderful.'

Chapter Two

Between them the two civil servants at the Cabinet Office had received many honours, something they both felt was their due. The more senior of them, Sir Kenneth Dunn, ran the Parole Board without, mercifully, ever having to face a prisoner or visit a prison, nor for that matter had his junior colleague, Sir Anthony Henderson. In Whitehall, however, they were regarded as the experts and the Prisons Minister sought their advice frequently. The two men often joked with each other that they thought the Justice Minister, their minister, should be locked up, given some of the views she came out with, not least her new idea that one of her senior civil servants should accompany her on prison visits, an idea they found more than unacceptable as they had made clear to her, though there was a steely look in her eyes that made them feel uncomfortable.

'Have you met this Elliot fellow before?' asked Henderson.

'I was present at his consecration in the Abbey. All something of a disaster as it turned out, and I always thought appointing a professor of philosophy to that post was a mistake anyway.'

'So why have you proposed him for this particular job? He doesn't live anywhere near Banklyn.'

'It's not that far. We came up with this idea as a means of protecting the Parole Board following a run of bad press attention. The decisions made were correct in the eyes of the Board but the "hang'em and flog'em" brigade, and especially hysterical females, didn't see it that way, the latter not minding anything done by Muslims of course, but if a man has but looked at a woman, then his balls should be removed at the very least.'

'Yes, I know exactly what you mean. I have a daughter-in-law who is an extremist too.'

'So we thought it would be a good idea to protect ourselves somewhat by appointing liaison officers between ourselves and the applicant for parole upon whom it would be possible to apportion a measure of responsibility if something went wrong. He or she would be an independent observer of the inmate upon whose recommendation we would rely and if by any chance something should go wrong and we release someone who immediately repeats their offence, we can always say we were badly advised.'

'Elliott's not your average do-gooder though and he's hardly stupid and will surely see through what you're suggesting.'

'From what I know about him, and I have received communication both from Cambridge and Lambeth, he's extremely weak when it comes to refusing appeals to his sense of duty. We shall have to appeal to his better nature and present it as something which is a cross between a challenge and a real opportunity to serve, which of course he has not been doing since his resignation from Truro.'

There was a knock on the door, followed by the appearance of the face of a secretary.

'Sir Kenneth, Dr Elliot is here.'

'Do bring him straight in, Helen, and enquire of him what he would like to drink, and perhaps you could bring our drinks in now too.'

'Of course.'

The men stood as Alex came into the room and they

introduced themselves before sitting.

'I'm not sure I can call you any more by your previous titles which were very grand, and grander than ours but would you be happy if I simply called you Alex?'

'Of course Sir Kenneth,' said Alex pointedly.

'Have you been in the Cabinet Office before? I'm sure you've been in number 10, presumably when you were appointed to Truro, but there's much less hustle and bustle here and to be perfectly honest I think we get more work done than across there. Our boss, the Cabinet Secretary, of maintains the link between us and endeavours to keep the measure of control over what happens there.'

'As far as I'm aware,' said Alex, 'we've now had two women prime ministers but as yet no female Cabinet Secretary.'

'I'm sure it will happen. The difference between ourselves and MPs is that they can come in at any stage in their career, whether properly qualified or not, whereas if you wish to rise to the top of the Civil Service, you have to make that decision early on and make a career of it. It sounds sexist, and no doubt there will be those who insist that it is, but it's extremely difficult for women to get to the top in the Service if they have to take time out for raising a family. It's simply a biological fact.'

The door opened and in came Helen with 3 cups of tea, milk and sugar, and each of the men took what they needed from her.'

'So to business,' said Sir Anthony. 'As a diocesan bishop you had an automatic right of entrance to any prison within your diocese.'

'I certainly did, only there weren't any, apart that is from Bodmin Gaol, a tourist attraction which closed as a prison in 1927.'

'Dartmoor?'

'No, it comes under the jurisdiction of the Bishop of Exeter, and I had no need ever to visit.'

'What about other prisons? Are you familiar with any?'

'If I was being facetious, which of course I'm not, I might suggest the Church of England, from which I escaped.'

The two civil servants laughed dutifully. Somewhat flustered, Sir Anthony continued.

'The Parole Board is a very important institution making decisions about when men and women are approaching the end of their sentence, with a view to releasing them under licence into the community provided they are no further risk. In itself that is a risky business and normally the Board takes at least six months to arrive at a decision. Sometimes it's straightforward. A history of good behaviour during a relatively short sentence will allow many to be released early though these too are closely examined before a decision is made. With some others it is a much more onerous responsibility. We are constantly trying to improve the system but nothing is perfect, so the suggestion has been made, and we both think it is a very good one, that there should be a liaison person between the Board, the prison staff, victims of their family and the prisoner, someone who can observe and talk to someone who is becoming eligible for parole at much the time when the application is being made. The liaison person will not be a member of the Board and therefore will have no responsibility for the final decision, but we anticipate his or her report to have great weight in the proceedings of the Board.

'It's for that reason that we are approaching and hopefully appointing those who will be willing to spend time inside endeavouring to learn what you can from staff and inmate alike. Each prison in the country will have such a liaison person with a stipend from the Department of Justice.'

'Isn't there a possibility that this liaison officer will simply end up as the fall guy if something goes wrong.'

Sir Kenneth intervened.

'A decision by the Parole Board is never reached without

extensive consideration of the case and consists of a judge, together with professional psychiatrists and psychologists and others, who receive reports not from one source but from a number, and it's on the totality that the decision is arrived at. The report from the liaison officer would offer a different and important perspective.'

'I've never been into a prison and I don't know much about penology or even the psychology of those who commit crimes. I'm therefore a little puzzled why you think I might be an appropriate person to go into Banklyn prison.'

I'm in great danger of flattering you, so I give that warning before I begin. Alex, other than in Lambeth Palace, you are thought of highly as one of the most principled men of your generation. You are highly intelligent with a strong sense of pastoral care. You are easy to talk to and of course, you are a family man and married to a very fine poet. You are exactly what we are looking for. You will go in with nothing known about your past as I gather just about everyone in prison is suspicious of religious zealots. In a way all we are asking is that you agree to go in there and listen. I know you have responsibilities with the National Park, but the real question to face is whether the time has now come for you to do something substantial in this way for the wider community.'

'I'm glad you weren't flattering me!'

The three of them laughed, and the civil servants realised they had won.

Two officers had accompanied Teddy to the Governor's office and he couldn't think why. The Parole Board process had hardly begun and to the best of his knowledge he had broken no rules nor assaulted another inmate, so as he stood there facing Mr Wilson, he was somewhat confused.

'I imagine you are wondering why you are here, Armstrong. It is however, related to your Board, and a new way in which they will be helped to make their decision by your seeing an independent person in the run-up to the decision-making process, who will be trying to get to know you and us better as we all strive to reach a decision about your application for parole. I know nothing about him other than that he is an experienced person and that he will be here next week, on Thursday. That's all. Take him back to his cell, Mr Bainbridge.'

'Yes sir.'

As he departed, into the office came the deputy governor Myles.

'Did he say anything?'

' I'm sure he regards it as another hoop to manipulate his way through, something at which he's very accomplished. I'll be interested to note what this Elliot chap picks up but to be perfectly honest I think it's a total waste of time and something the Parole Board have come up with as a way of protecting their arses. However we will help in any way we can and that I'm afraid, will involve you, Myles. When he gets here on Thursday morning you will need to do an induction course with him, and show him around generally, and answer any questions he has about the place or about Armstrong. We should all try to be friendly because his face will become quite familiar as there will be others after Armstrong. The chances are that he'll be some sort of trendy leftie who thinks they should all be let out but we shall see. By the way he will have full Parole Board rights and can therefore see anything and everything relating to the prisoner.'

'Will you be here, Andy?'

'Certainly and I think it will be a good idea if we arranged a lunch for the senior staff and Mr Elliot, as we do when other PB people come. Perhaps you would so kind as let Rev Smallwood know the arrangements for the day as the Liaison Officer should include a visit to the Chapel as part of his induction. Mind you

Myles, if no one is listening and I have not said this officially, but I seriously wonder whether we should be letting these religious professionals into our prisons. It could be argued that what they are doing is corrupting the minds of those in a vulnerable position just as we all know the wretched imams do when they come in to see the Moslems.'

'Have you ever been religious?'

'No. When I was young my hobby was fishing and although I think religion is just a hobby too, it's considerably more dangerous than fishing.'

'Unless of course you're a fish!'

Although her former young fans were no longer quite so keen on her now that she had completely changed her style of poetry, Emily continued to receive invitations to do readings. The twins provided her with the perfect excuse when she chose to turn something down, but an acceptance meant an outing for the whole family, including the twins and also her mum, Amy, to whom both Emily and Alex were particularly close. They saw a lot of her as she loved to come to spend a day with the twins, and longer if at all possible. Today they were on their way to the Hay Festival where Emily had done readings in the past. On this occasion she would have two appearances, one to read some of her latest work and a second, to be interviewed on stage by Ella Gorham, which would be recorded by the BBC and played on some still to be decided occasion. Emily was especially looking forward to seeing Nicky, her publisher who might be there with Claire, and selling lots of copies of her book as well as being on the scout for outstanding new writers. In his days at the Poetry House Oliver had come every year and always enjoyed himself.

They had booked themselves into a hotel describing itself as "child-friendly" and happily it proved to be so. Amy would take care of the twins during the day allowing Alex and Emily to attend the festival which meant that everyone was happy, George and Chloe adoring their granny! Emily's reading seemed to be going very well until there was a kind of protest. A group of young people started shouting that she had "sold out" to the forces of the political right. For just a few moments it felt as if things were getting out of hand, but stewards were quickly on hand to shepherd them away. Alex was sitting at the side of the stage and wondered whether he should go out to Emily, but he recognised that she needed no help and simply waited patiently for the handful of protesters to be moved away. Then she continued to warm applause from those present.

After lunch in her radio interview Ella Gorham raised the matter of the protest and asked whether it had bothered her.

'I've been racking my brain,' she said, 'trying to recall if there has ever been such a protest before – you know, complaining that a poet has changed his or her style, neophobia, and I can't think of any, so I shall definitely take that as a plus. I didn't mind it in the slightest and once it was over, I simply continued with what I was doing, but what concerned me was that it is a sign of the increasing politicisation of art and of the growth of intolerance. Increasingly when I go to an art exhibition I feel as if I am being assaulted in the name of someone's political prejudices, and I'm certainly less keen to subject myself to that than when I was younger. I know some say all art is by its very nature political and would include my poetry. If I thought that was so, then I would stop writing and give all my time over to caring for my children. I read English at Oxford and encountered enough literary theory to last me a lifetime, and it's why I no longer do readings in universities just in case I'm not politically acceptable and my audience consists solely of snowflakes.'

Nicky and Claire were waiting with Alex for Emily to leave the stage.

'Emily, I've published everything of yours including both so-called styles and I can honestly say neither your more recent work nor the earlier was political in any kind of narrow sense. I know that some poetry now is explicitly so, that's not how it is with yours and as your publisher I endorse all you said. As your friend, I love you.'

'Thank you, Nicky.'

Alex came and kissed his wife.

'I love you too.'

She smiled.

'We should be getting back to Chloe and George.'

'Of course,' said Nicky, 'but let's have a cup of tea first.'

'Ah,' added Claire, 'priority for the English everywhere: a cup of tea!'

Chapter Three

The Rev Angus Smallwood arrived home and the first thing he did was to consult his copy of *Crockford's Clerical Directory*, which listed everyone in the Church of England who had been ordained, and there he was: Alexander George Elliot, Lord Bishop of Truro, though he was so no more. So this was what bishops did when they left the Church, apart, that is, from marrying a young and beautiful poet. He wondered what the governor would think if he knew who was coming, given that Andy was not entirely sympathetic to the cause of religion. Then again, neither was Angus Smallwood. He hung on only by working outside parish and diocesan structures as a prison chaplain and was enjoying his time in Banklyn where there were not too many comings and goings. Previously he had been a chaplain in a local prison with arrivals and departures daily, and where there had been big problems with drugs, many of which were passed round during the Sunday service in the chapel. It was different here and security considerably tighter. The governor may not have liked religion but Angus knew that he was good at his job.

Many of those with whom he had to deal on a day-to-day basis were serving life sentences, meaning in practice anything from 20 to 30 years, and some were serving whole life sentences, which meant that they would be imprisoned until they died. He knew some of them very well. He was sometimes asked whether he felt fear in the presence of those who had done terrible things, and whilst that might have been the case when he began this work, it was not so now. He was however, sometimes horrified if he needed to read a prisoner's file and discovered what he had done. There was a team of psychological and psychiatric workers with whom he tried to liaise, and although there were some inmates whom he felt might well have now repented and reformed, there were others for whom this seemed to be a total impossibility.

And now the liaison officer, formerly the Bishop of Truro, would be coming regularly to offer a personal assessment on Teddy Armstrong and, presumably, others as the possibility of parole arose. He didn't know Teddy particularly well as he kept himself very much to himself. He had been assuming that Teddy would sail through the parole process for it seemed to him no matter how he had been before being sent down he had unquestionably learned self-control, and if he could manage that inside with daily provocations, surely he might do the same outside. Anyway, he very much looked forward to meeting Dr Elliot.

Alex took the train to Beverley on Wednesday afternoon, and then a cab to a small hotel in the delightful town, and having settled in to his room walked out to see the racecourse which looked so well looked after and cared for as much as many of the Thoroughbreds than raced there. After feasting on a curry, he spent the evening divided between reading his papers on the PB, and speaking to Emily on his mobile.

Waking early, Alex had a shower and then spoke to Emily, who reported that when they came into her bed the twins were both confused by daddy's absence.

'Make sure you tell them daddy will be there when they come in tomorrow.'

'I already have done but they're especially delighted that granny is here.'

'Make sure you give her my love and I will call later.'

'I hope it goes well, my darling.'

'Me too!'

After breakfast a taxi took him through to Banklyn. The prison officers on the gates were expecting him but he still had to produce his official papers before they allowed him inside. He was required to be searched and sniffed for drugs by the spaniel on duty. The officer in charge told him he would be given a set of keys after he had completed the induction. He was led to the offices of the deputy governor and looking about him he could see all the paraphernalia of high security. No one had even attempted to escape from here and it was hardly surprising.

Myles received and welcomed Alex and over the compulsory cup of tea explained the format of the morning ahead, that it would be followed by lunch with the senior staff. They then set about the business of understanding the ethos of the place and its inmates. Alex received instruction on how to respond to being taken hostage and the measures he should take to avoid it (he was suddenly not quite so keen to do the job!). Being a Category A prison, he was introduced to a number of important safety devices and emergency switches and buttons and informed as to the location of the armoury. He then showed Alex some workshops in which the men spent their time and the library where some, but only some, had access to computers, though Myles pointed out that there were powerful filters on all the machines, and all webpages were monitored by staff. He then led him through to the chapel and left him in the hands of Angus Smallwood.

'Welcome Dr Elliot, which I guess is the right way to address you. I'm the full-time Anglican chaplain here and although I function in York archdiocese and have a licence, I'm only answerable to the Justice Department, but I'm sure you are well aware of that kind of thing.'

'Not really, Angus. This is the first I've ever been inside a prison.'

'Then I think it's called starting at the top. This is the government's pride and joy.'

'How long have you been here?'

'Six years, and before that I was at the nick in Leeds. They're totally different, this being the place where on a day-to-day basis my parishioners are pretty constant and usually here for a long time.'

'Do you enjoy your job?'

'Working here is a constant challenge. Some, and it includes Islamic terrorists, have done things which are evil and I'm convinced from what I know of them, were they to be released they would almost certainly repeat them. For others, the end of their time marks the possibility of a new beginning, though between you and me I'm pessimistic about that.'

'Isn't that dispiriting?'

'I've never thought of myself as a moral improver and if I did I'd be bitterly disappointed. If you come regularly, you ought to know that even worse than illegal drugs, though that's not too much of a problem here, is the culture of deceit. All prisoners will lie to get what they want and they do it all the time. If they tell you something be very wary and preferably don't believe it. Believe me, if no one else today, that I'm not being cynical. They will all try it on. Those of us who work here all the time know this but when people come for the first time, like you today, underestimating the acting ability of inmates could be very dangerous indeed. Sometimes the Parole Board are hoodwinked and someone who most definitely shouldn't be is released.'

Alex laughed.

'So I don't imagine you give much of your sermon time over to telling them to be better boys. But how would you describe your job?'

'With great difficulty. There is a service every Sunday, and the local Roman priest comes in as well every month. An Imam from Hull comes quite often, too often I think, and it's my job to facilitate their visits. There are certain statutory duties I have to fulfil which include visiting any prisoners in isolation or the hospital wing and seeing all new arrivals, though there aren't that many, whereas at Leeds there were usually at least thirty daily. I also try to take seriously the care and support for the staff, many of whom find the church "out there" irrelevant and impossible.'

'As I went round with Myles, I didn't notice any women. Is that because it would be too dangerous for them to work here?'

'Oh no. We have plenty women working here, including female prison officers, almost all of whom I think could take care of themselves if necessary. There is the secretarial staff and most of the psychological and psychiatric staff are women too. Between you and me, Dr Elliot, one or two of the female officers almost certainly play rugby on their days off.'

'Yes, well, women's rugby is being played everywhere now.'

'Who said anything about women's rugby?'

The two men looked at each other and grinned.

'I go back to my original question,' said Alex, 'do you enjoy your job?'

'If I say yes, then that's because it's the last outpost of being in the Church I can can continue to occupy, if you take my meaning.'

Alex smiled again.

'I think I do.'

'I have to confess to finding out more about you than we have been told officially. To my mind you're still on the side of the angels, and if any wish to be confirmed, I'll know who to send for.'

'I could never make sense of confirmation even whilst I was doing them, so perhaps you should consult the Bishop of Hull.'

'Hmm. He and I don't see eye to eye on much. He thinks I should be organising evangelistic campaigns in here and setting up *Alpha* groups and he keeps angling for a visit and I always say No.'

'That's greatly to your credit, believe you me,' said Alex.

'Before I take you through to lunch, Myles has left me a form for you to sign. These days you no longer have to sign the Official Secrets Act to be bound by it, but the Justice Department would prefer you to do so.'

Alex signed the form.

After a tedious lunch with members of staff, the governor himself, plus an officer, led Alex to a cell which was opened for him and the key turned again after opening so the bolt remained active preventing the door being slammed shut with Alex still inside. Alex was feeling decidedly uneasy as he entered the cell and met Teddy Armstrong for the first time. He sat on a chair, Armstrong on his bed.

Armstrong looked perfectly normal and gave Alex a smile which he did not feel he could return..

'Good afternoon, sir,' Armstrong began. 'I'm pleased you're here so that in some way you might play a part in my release by the Board.'

'As you know I'm not a member of the Board but simply a liaison person between the staff, yourself, the parents of the victims and those who will serve on the Board. Anything I report will have no greater weight than that of any other professional involved.'

'Yes, but unlike them, you will have met and know me.'

'Your doctors do and the prison officials.'

Armstrong smiled the sort of smile that said a lot without a word being spoken and indicated what he thought of the "professionals".

'Did you expect 20 years?'

'I expected 30 and so did my brief.'

'And you've spent most of that time in Wakefield and here.'

'I was on remand and for the length of the trial in Manchester. Then they moved me to Wakefield.'

'I gather that if the Parole Board says yes to your application, you will first be moved to an Open Prison and released from there.'

'Yeah, well, I have asked to be released from here. There would be no protection there for anyone sentenced for my crime.'

'You admit that you did it?'

'I have never denied that as you will see from the transcript of my trial. I pleaded guilty. That probably accounts for it just being 20 years.'

'Do you ever reflect on the fact that at one time you would have been hanged for what you did?'

'At one time anyone stealing a sheep would be hanged. We've moved on, not that I don't know there will be a lot of people out there who would wish it for me.'

'So, after all this time, what do you now think about what you did to those children?'

Armstrong sat silently for a while.

'What I did was terrible beyond the capacity of words to describe. To say that "I wasn't myself" is ludicrous because obviously I was and if I could turn back the clock, I genuinely think I would drown myself rather than do it again because I'm the one who should have died, not them. I can't put it right and to say that I am and always will be ashamed is meaningless, said only to make myself imagine that it could make me feel better. It can't.'

'If your application is successful, what do you envisage as your lifestyle? I gather that your family disowned you at the time of the trial and have continued to indicate that they wish no further contact with you, and finding friends in your situation will not be easy, so what are you going to do?'

'The Justice Department, which didn't exist when I came inside, has told me that I will be given a new identity, birth certificate and passport, though as I shall be on licence there will be no opportunity to go abroad. I'm not being allowed to go anywhere near the Lake District but I have indicated that I would like to be considered for resettlement in the Derbyshire Dales and Peak District.'

Alex at once felt uneasy.

'I have acquired a degree from the OU in here in Computing and IT and so if I'm looking for work it will be in that general field, offering to mend computers and that sort of thing. I shall be living in a hostel at first, hopefully in Derby.'

'You give me the impression of being very open and straight in what you have told me. There are a number of other things which I think we should explore on the occasion of my next visit here.'

Armstrong laughed.

'However many times we meet I very much hope to convince you that what you see is what you get.'

Alex stood up, took out his keys, and without a backward glance, turned back the bolt on the locking mechanism of the door and then closed it behind him locking it from outside. Through the anti-suicide net he could see a number of inmates helping themselves to a cup of tea from an urn, supervised by two officers, one of whom was unquestionably one of the rugby playing females! He walked along the gantry to the gate and let himself out from the wing, making his way back to the governor's office. Andy stood up as Alex walked in and directed him to a seat, informing him that the inevitable beverage was on its way.

'How did it go?' asked Andy.

'You will all be much more used to it than I am,' replied Alex, 'but I found it almost impossible to get past my knowledge of what he did to those children all those years ago.'

'You're wrong. I don't think any of us who have looked through the files, find it easy to overlook what we know. My staff are professional and sometimes we have to work very hard to maintain the standards required of us when we are in the presence of those, and there are many of them here, whose crimes are utterly despicable. Some of them will be here until death and I would be dishonest if I didn't say I am glad of that, however ghastly being in prison is. Others like your man want to get out and have a second chance. Making a recommendation of that is an extremely frightening business and I never do it lightly, but I shall be very interested to hear what you have to say about your time with Armstrong this afternoon.'

'He is immediately plausible and seems to have realised that his best hope lies in a frank admission of a terrible deed in the past and a claim to integrity in the present. Is he playing the system?'

'To have picked up that from one visit is impressive. I would say the same and so, I think, would most of the staff, including those responsible for his psychological assessment, but to think that, even to be convinced, is not the same as being able to prove it. That point will be picked up by his legal representative at the Board, I'm sure.'

'There's something you could help me with. Armstrong was sentenced to 20 years and now the 20 years is up. Why is he not being automatically released?'

'Because he wasn't sentenced to 20 years. He was sentenced to life imprisonment and the judge recommended that he serve a minimum of 20 years before he is considered for parole. That's not always made totally clear on television. If he fails to get parole, and continues to do so every time he applies, he will remain here serving his life sentence for abduction, rape and murder until his life ends.

'Thank you Andy. Now you say it I feel rather stupid.'

'The law is a strange creature sometimes. In Armstrong's case a great deal will hang on the Victim's Statements which I have no doubt they will want to deliver in person and I very much doubt if they will pull any punches. You've seen some of the letters they have sent him.'

'Yes, Myles showed me them. And I believe I shall have to go and pay them a visit. Well, I think that's all I need to be doing today. I will just say though, that my admiration for you and your staff is enormous. Thank you for what you do.'

Alex handed in his keys before the main doors were opened and outside waas waiting for him the taxi that had been called. In no time at all he was on the platform at Beverley station waiting for his train. In less than an hour and a half Emily or Amy would be waiting to collect him and take him home. Standing there he decided not to pursue a life of crime.

Chapter Four

It was about an hour out from Beverley that Alex began to feel that something was the matter but he had no idea what it was. He felt strangely dizzy and voices around him seemed exaggerated and echoing, but most alarming of all was the fact that he began to feel anxious and agitated. He had felt nothing like this before. He could sense that he was perspiring heavily and that his heart was beating considerably faster than usual. Perhaps it was something he had eaten at lunchtime which wasn't agreeing with him. He stood and slowly made his way towards the end of the carriage and took out his phone and pressed his "help" keys, a shortcut they had programmed into their phones, the call being answered by Emily. Immediately she sensed that something was not right and urged him to go back to his seat and told him that she and the twins would leave immediately for the station even though Amy was already on her way.

He was now feeling worse than ever and when he sat down again, the young woman opposite asked him if he needed help of any sort as he didn't look well. He was barely able to reply, and the woman at once got out of her seat to find the guard. When the pair came back Alex was barely conscious. The guard looked at Alex's ticket on the seat next to him.

'He's going to Sheffield. I'll call ahead and get an ambulance. I should think he needs to be in hospital and I can't see much point in stopping the train before then because any ambulance that came would take him to Sheffield anyway.'

The woman nodded.

'I can't smell any alcohol and I don't know enough about drugs to know whether he's taken any, but I can't think he's the sort who would,' she said.

'I agree, but he doesn't look good.'

By this time Alex was wholly unaware of what was happening. In the meantime the guard was on his mobile and forewarning the staff at Sheffield that they should call an emergency ambulance for one of his customers.

At the station there was an ambulance with blue lights on the platform waiting for the arrival of the train though Amy was oblivious to this as she sat in her car as she sat listening to the radio. She therefore received a rude awakening by the utterly unexpected sight of arrival of Emily knocking urgently on her window.

'Mum, Alex has been taken ill on the train. Can you take my car and the twins home?'

'Of course. Give me your keys. Let me know.'

She ran to the car with its sleeping occupants and set off at once. Emily went on to the platform. Two green-suited paramedics were clearly waiting for the train to arrive and had with them a stretcher on wheels. Emily approached them.

'Do you know who it is you're waiting for? My husband called me to say he was not well.'

'We have no name, love. The guard called it in. Whoever it is has been unconscious for a while now and we'll need to get him or her to hospital as soon as possible.'

The train was now approaching. A man in a uniform was waving to the paramedics from an open door which meant he had access to the mechanism and so must be the guard. The paramedics boarded the train but a lot of people were getting off, making it difficult for Emily to get on. Eventually she made it to where she could see the paramedics at work with someone on the carriage floor. As she drew near, there was no doubt: it was Alex.

One of the paramedics looked up towards her.

'Is it him?' she asked.

'Yes,' said Emily. 'He's my husband, Alex Elliot.'

It took a while for Alex to be moved to the ambulance. It seemed to Emily that he was unconscious throughout and she was desperate for them to get on with it and get him to hospital. They worked on him for a further ten minutes inside the ambulance. At last the doors were closed and the woman paramedic came over to Emily.

'We're taking your husband to the Northern General as they're doing the emergency rota this evening.'

'But it's much further away than the Hallamshire.'

'We'll have blue lights and the siren on so it won't take long. Please don't try to keep up with us as that could be dangerous. When you get to A&E go to the Reception desk as they'll need information from you, and then someone will come for you.'

Three times in the next two hours Emily went to make enquiries and received exactly the same reply that someone would come. She had telephoned Amy and said that as soon as she had some news she would keep her informed and in the meantime, she imagined the worst and how she was going to manage without Alex, bringing up the children with her mum alongside her. So it was with a considerable measure of relief that she saw coming towards her a young man casually dressed with what used to be called a "baby face" that made him look far younger than he probably was, very much like the physicist and celebrity, Brian Cox.

'Mrs Elliot? I'm Peter Swainson, the A&E consultant.'

'Really? – oh I'm sorry I don't mean to be rude.'
He smiled.
'Don't worry about it. I sometimes get asked if I've done my GCSEs yet, and then when I tell them I've got a wife and three children, they mostly assume I must have started very early indeed. It so happens, however, that it's true. My wife's a GP and we did med school together, and I think we must both have been missing on the morning they were teaching us about contraception. And your husband tells me you've got twins.'

'So he's conscious?'

'He is, though at the moment he's been taken for a brain scan, but he'll be back soon. Come on through and wait for him.'

Dr Swainson led the way through a number of swing doors and then, turning right, they went into a unit containing a number of bays, almost all of which were occupied. He took her to the last bay on the right which contained all sorts of equipment and an empty bed. Dr Swainson moved a chair for her to sit on whilst he perched on the edge of the bed.

'I'm only guessing, and that's why we have scans, but I have a feeling that we shall find nothing other than the brain of a very clever man. There are no symptoms or signs of any abnormal brain activity, and all the other tests we've done have produced results which reveal no abnormality of the heart and other vital organs. When I last saw him he was engaging in what I imagine is normal conversation and above all expressing his overwhelming concern for you and your children, as well as your mother, of whom he's obviously very fond. I think it's not unrealistic to describe what happened as a panic attack, but that can cover a multitude of things. If the scans are clear, I can see no reason why he cannot return home tonight, but… something happened on the train, something you, he and we do not want repeated, so we shall have to make an out-patients appointment for him even if, at this precise moment, I'm not sure exactly which department we are talking about.

'I gather he had been spending the day in Banklyn high security prison near Hull, doing work for the Parole Board. He will have come across some pretty awful individuals. It's possible that in some way he was overwhelmed by the experience. If so he perhaps ought to consider stopping. I can't imagine that it's a bundle of fun. Anyway the most important thing is that I can happily sign him off and send him home to your tender care. By the way, I've seen you before.'

'Oh?'

'It was on YouTube. You did a reading on the Bill Maher show in Los Angeles, probably a day or so before you and your husband were killed in the plane crash, as we were all informed at the time. I watch Bill every week and I remember Emily Cunningham very well indeed. You were quite a hit.'

'Thank you for that, but thank you even more for your care and concern for both Alex and me.'

This was a very busy department with a lot of activity. Emily sat there almost mesmerised by it all and then, to her absolute delight, wearing hospital pyjamas and dressing gown, Alex appeared. She rushed to him and flung her arms around him.

'Hey,' he said, 'you need to take care, I'm an invalid.'

'No you're not, you old rogue, and with a bit of luck we will soon be on our way home, but in the meantime sit down on the bed and tell me everything.'

He described all that had happened on the train, but could remember nothing after that until he was aware that he was in a hospital with people around him doing tests, having an x-ray and so on. According to the doctor they showed nothing to cause any concern and so he sent me for a brain scan to see if I had possibly had a stroke, but the radiologist on duty said there were no signs of anything untoward.

'They are of course concerned about what happened, not least because they want to do everything they can to make sure it doesn't happen again, so I imagine they will ask me to come back as an outpatient.'

'Yes Dr Swainson said the same to me, though he wasn't altogether clear which discipline it should come under.'

'But tell me about you, and the children and Amy – you are all much more important than me.'

'Don't be silly. They're fine. Mum was due to meet you at the station but when I got your call I came in with the children and she took them back home.'

'I can't remember calling you.'

'You did. It scared the living daylights out of me.'

'I'm sorry about that, my darling.'

One of the sisters in her dark blue uniform came into the bay.

'I gather the radiologist gave you the good news so there's nothing to stop you getting dressed and going home. You will receive an appointment through the post for outpatients and it may be here or at the Hallamshire, though it goes without saying that you will get far better treatment if you come here. But I'm glad we've been able to be of some service to you and we all hope that whatever happened isn't repeated. One final thing, you mustn't drive for 48 hours. There's no obligation to inform the DVLA about this. If it was repeated then there might be. I've also got some information here for you about how to monitor your activity and behaviour after such an event. Okay?'

'Thank you very much, sister, and to all your staff.'

As she left the bay, she pulled the curtains across to allow him to get dressed. As they left Dr Swainson waved to them from the bedside of another patient. By the looks of things he was in for a busy night.

Emily had decided that on the journey home their conversation should consist primarily of banalities, accounts of what the children had been doing during the day and what they had been doing with Amy. She did not want him to tell her about his visit to the prison, nor did she repeat to him the words of Dr Swainson about abandoning it.

By the time they arrived home Alex was looking pretty awful and not saying a great deal other than to greet and thank Amy. When asked if he wanted some food he replied that the only thing he wanted was sleep and in a matter of minutes he was upstairs and in bed, having first looked in on the sleeping children.

Emily came into the sitting room with a plate of cold food prepared by her mum and sat down beside her.

'Did the doctor say anything to you as to why he thought it might have happened?' asked Amy.

'On the whole they are baffled as there is no obvious physical cause, but something did happen, something the consultant thought could be described as a panic attack and I would say, knowing and loving him as I do, something is still happening inside him. I suspect we may be talking about something triggered by whatever happened or whatever he saw or heard when he was in prison, and whatever else the future holds for him I'm far from convinced that he should ever go back, but you know what he's like when it comes to duty. That was how he got into the mess of becoming a priest in Cambridge, and even more, a bishop in Cornwall. I know better than anyone that Alex is an extremely complicated person but I'm going to be there for him and with him if there are matters that have to be faced.'

'I've sometimes thought,' said Amy, 'that he has lost something precious, much like it would be for a sailor, long before the advent of modern technology, who lost his sextant overboard. He can go on sailing but really has no overall sense of direction. Might it be that his experiences earlier today have brought that home to him in an extremely powerful way. Without his spiritual identity, maybe today was more than he could cope with.'

'But does that imply that I'm not enough for him, that I'm not to him what he is to me?'

'Not at all. If I can pursue the analogy, you are the boat, not just protecting but also sustaining him and without you, George and Chloe, and dare I say, me too, he would sink. Now, my love, I may have got this completely and utterly wrong but I have to say that Alex does not seem to me to be someone with mental health difficulties, but I do think he has spiritual health difficulties, even impossibilities. You, on the other hand, have full expression to your spiritual needs through your poetry, much as the other man in your life, also a senior clergyman, John Donne, also had.'

Emily smiled.

'Yes, I forget just how much. Perhaps I should have headed notepaper with the words: Emily Elliot – Corrupter of Clergy (no one below the level of a Dean should apply).'

Emily sighed deeply before she continued.

'It's worth thinking about. Quite what the man in bed upstairs will think of it, I just don't know, though it does occur to me that if anyone could broach the matter with him, it would have to be you, because I know how much he respects you and the things you say about what you both call the spiritual life. He would think I was being cynical if I was to say any of this, but he would know that you would never be cynical about such matters. I know it sounds silly but I'm sometimes quite jealous of your relationship with Alex and this is the very area where I feel I have no admission, that it is very special and important but belongs only to you two.'

'Put at its simplest, Em, I used to be a nun and your husband used to be a bishop, and I can't ever remember you being even remotely religious. For your husband and me it's like two people living abroad and having to speak a foreign language all the time, who when they meet are able to speak English with one another. That's all, and you know I don't actually go to church any more than Alex does, but that's not the same as possessing a spiritual sextant which for one reason or another has disappeared. But I do know this on the basis of many years observation and experience, including that of your father and me, I have never known any man love and adore his life partner, more than Alex loves you.'

'And that is how it was with John Donne and his wife. How I wish I could write love poetry like his!'

Little children are no respecters of the lunacy of their parents and therefore roused Alex from his sleep shortly after five o'clock. He gathered them safely in his arms and took them downstairs and warmed some of Emily's milk which they drank with relish. Having burped them he placed them in their baby-bouncers and then one after the other changed their nappies. He now moved them to their 'gym' which they loved with all its colours, faces and noises. As he sat looking at them he was thinking about what had happened yesterday and so intent was he that he didn't hear his mother-in-law come in until she sat next to him on the sofa.

'You're up early, Amy.'

The children caught sight of granny and made noises of approval, and she went over and spoke to them which increased the volume of their approval. She returned to the sofa.

'To be honest, Alex, I haven't really slept all that well, mainly because of you.'

'In which case I can only apologise but if it's any consolation, apart from still feeling very tired there are no signs of whatever it was that happened to me yesterday.'

'I'm glad of that but to be perfectly honest it wasn't your physical state as such that troubled my night, but something else completely. Em said they would be sending you an outpatients appointment and I wouldn't be at all surprised if it was to see a psychologist or psychiatrist because that's how they will think about what happened to you on the train given that they have excluded any actual physical causes. It's totally up to you to decide whether you cancel or keep that appointment but if you were to ask me, and you probably won't, though I'll tell you anyway, if you keep that appointment you will be wasting your time and theirs. You really don't need a shrink of any sort nor to find yourself wrapped up in long-term therapy. I could understand that someone in your position might find that a temptation, and given that you've a fascinating history, a therapist would salivate in anticipation. But Alex, you do not need that.'

'I'm glad to hear it.'

Chloe had decided that the most enjoyable thing she could do in the gym this morning was to hit her brother, so Alex picked her up and sat her on his knee which is probably what she wanted all along. George was delighted now to be king of the castle and continued to play happily. With Chloe in his arms the possibilities of continuing the conversation with Amy were now likely to be limited.

'I think I'll get on with their breakfast,' said Amy. 'It's a bit early I know but they won't object.'

Amy went through to the kitchen and began preparing the porridge for George and Chloe and put on some toast for Alex and herself. In the meantime and much to her delight, Chloe had daddy all to herself and was loving it. After breakfast Amy said she would take them upstairs and get them dressed, leaving Alex to do some thinking.

'Whereabouts are you, for you look miles away?' said his favourite voice in all the world.

He turned towards the door and saw before him a vision of loveliness that had not yet attended to its hair, not unlike Botticelli's Venus!

'I'm here and completely yours, plus the others obviously.'

'Chloe and George were awake early I take it.'

'Round about 5 o'clock I think and I didn't want them to wake you, so I got up and gave them some milk and I've been here ever since, having half a conversation with your mum and anticipating the second half sometime soon.'

'I wasn't listening in by the way, but she and I had a short chat last night and I think I know what she wanted to say, even if I have no idea whether it's the right thing. But I trust my mum and even if you choose to lay aside what she has to say, I still think you should listen.'

'You know how high an opinion I have of her so I would never reject anything she said without having given it proper attention.'

Emily came and sat next to Alex and took his hand.

'You scared the living daylights out of me yesterday, and inevitably I began thinking how I would manage as a single parent and what sort of financial arrangements there are in place, and all sorts of things like that.'

'I feel absolutely fine this morning, the hospital thought I was fine last night, but I thought I might be dying when it happened.'

'I don't suppose you've been able to give any thought yet whether you go on with this Parole Board business, but if that was a contributing factor, you will need to consider your future in it.'

'I think it's involved in some way, but I saw nothing untoward, and no one said anything awful, and the prisoner I had to see could not have been better behaved, so it's not going to be straightforward trying to unravel the knot.'

'Are you able to pull out if you chose to do so?'

'In my life so far I've pulled out of being a professor, I've pulled out of being a bishop, and, you may remember, I pulled out of being a companion to a poet on an American tour and became instead her lover and then her fiancée and later her husband. So pulling out of something organised by the Cabinet Office will be easy in comparison.'

'You are very annoying, Alexander Elliot. I was trying to have a serious conversation and now you've set my heart a-flutter with all sorts of wonderful memories. I can't talk any more, I just want to hug and kiss you.'

'I don't think I'll pull out of that!'

Amy was returning to her home on the edge of Sheffield but before setting off helped Alex put the children into their cots in the hope of a mid-morning sleep. It was his day for child care but at this precise moment he could quite happily have joined one or other of his children in a cot and gone straight to sleep.

'I mentioned to Emily that my PC is neither receiving nor sending emails and she said she would take over the twins at about three this afternoon, meaning that you could perhaps pop over and mend it.'

'Of course. It'll be straightforward, I'm sure.'

Emily and Alex fed the twins in their high chairs together and tried to talk.

'Were you aware,' asked Alex of his wife, 'that I have a PhD from Cambridge University?'

'You may have mentioned it.'

'And were you aware that, as a professor, I supervised others working for a PhD, and was external examiner for the same degree in a number of other universities?'

'I'm not sure. It must've slipped my mind.'

'Ah, well that will account for why it is that my wife and my mother-in-law think I'm the ideal person to change a setting on her computer that she would know perfectly well how to do. In other words, it's just a ploy to make me listen to what she has to say.'

'Gosh. The thought never occurred to me.'

Chloe had discovered the enormous fun there was in dropping grapes from her high chair to the ground and making mummy pick them up, and being a quick learner, George began to imitate his sister. Their chairs, their faces, their bibs and the floor were now covered with bits and pieces of what they had been trying to eat. Emily stood up.

'What a mess. I'm ever so glad it's not my day for childcare. Never mind clever Dr Elliot, with a first-class mind like yours clearing up this mess should be a doddle. I'll see you at about 3 o'clock.'

She kissed the twins and then gave her husband a particularly wonderful kiss, which both enjoyed, and at which the children stared. As she left the room to return to work, at least she knew that he knew about the plot to make him sit down with Amy, though if truth be told, he would not think that a great hardship.

Chapter Five

Amy's sofa had to be the most comfortable in the world, and whilst she made the tea, he stretched out on it and could quite easily have fallen fast asleep. Neither of them mentioned her computer on his arrival, for if anything it was more likely that he would call upon her for help with his own computer.

'This is a sponge cake from *Betty's* in Harrogate. My friend Marjorie went there two days ago and brought it back for me as a gift for no reason which is always the best sort of gift. Seeing you stretched out there suggests to me that you're feeling pretty weary.'

'I am. A day with the children is of course wonderful but utterly exhausting and not calculated to best help me get my thoughts in order. Even now I am struggling to make sense of what happened yesterday. Nothing like that has ever occurred before and I was rather disappointed that the hospital couldn't find a cause. It probably sounds silly but I think I could have coped with it more easily if they'd said I'd had a TIA – a mini-stroke, because at least then I would have some sort of understanding and presumably the doctors would have been able to tell me what to do to make sure it didn't happen again. So I'm totally at a loss.'

'Yes, it must have been so very frightening, especially on top of your time inside a prison housing some of the most dangerous and unpleasant of people. How much contact with them did you have?'

'I saw some at a distance, though I couldn't identify any, and the only one I spoke to was the one who is applying for parole.'

'Has he been there a long time?'

'Other than when he was on remand and during his trial, he has spent the last 20 years in Wakefield and more recently in Banklyn.'

'Are you allowed to tell me what he did?'

'It was in all the newspapers and on television so it's no great secret. He kidnapped two small sisters, raped and murdered them.'

Amy remained silent for a moment.

'Will any account be taken of the parents or other members of their family in the parole process?'

'Oh yes. At the beginning of the meeting of the Board they will be invited to make a statement, and it's totally up to them whether the prisoner is present or not. And now in addition to that, one of my roles is to go and see them and listen to them.'

'I can imagine that for them 20 years will seem a small price he has had to pay but did you talk with the prisoner about what he had done?'

'Not really, though he tried to convince me that he is utterly repentant. He won't want the details of what he did to be part of the parole process I imagine, realising that it would not work in his favour. His actual sentence was life imprisonment, but the judge specified that parole could be considered after a minimum of 20 years.'

'You know Alex, this was your first entry into a world populated by those who have done terrible things to others, which some understandably call evil. It's hardly surprising that it would have a powerful effect upon someone as sensitive as you.

If that lay behind what happened on the train then it was fully understandable. I can only imagine that it doesn't happen to those who go into the prison every day because they have to cut off from the forefront of their minds what they know, otherwise they couldn't do it or would themselves resort to murder, and I can imagine that it might make them hard.

'Perhaps you might decide not to go on with this work but even were you to do so, I think that what happened yesterday revealed something very important.'

'Go on.'

'Can you recall the name of Donald Crowhurst who took part in the Round the World Boat Race in 1969? He became completely lost in the Southern Atlantic, whilst still reporting and recording false positions in his log, pretending to be still taking part in the race. When his boat was found it was empty, and the evidence suggested a complete mental breakdown leading to suicide. I'm not suggesting that you are anywhere near that but it came to my mind.

'Yesterday's trauma, I suggest and as I said to Em, was caused by the fact that you no longer have any sort of compass or sextant by which to navigate. With Emily, Chloe and George you are safely settled of course, but there's considerably more to you than just being a beloved husband and daddy, wonderful though you are at both. But you've been both a Professor of Philosophy and a Diocesan Bishop, both of which are concerned more than anything else with meaning and whilst you discovered that neither could provide you with it, I can't believe that the quest has been completely abandoned.'

'When I met and fell in love with Emily I found the meaning I was looking for, and now there are the children and you. There is absolutely no way I could ever go back to the Church of England, and no way they'd have me, and I regret to say that philosophy is now so sterile I have no desire to return there either. And all things considered I do think this job with the Parole Board is worth doing.'

'I think you need some space, Alex, not by going away from home, but space at home. It's wonderful that you are so closely involved in caring for the children so much, allowing Em to work, but you should be giving thought to a childminder or a nanny for, say, three hours each weekday morning. It goes without saying that I will always do what I can with regard to my grandchildren – as I try to do now, but I'm getting older and in the next couple of years they are going to be more of a handful than they are now, once they start walking and getting up to mischief, so if what I'm suggesting were to take place, it would allow you a modicum of space to think and read, and Emily to continue to work.'

'We've never wanted to farm out the children.'

'Of course not, but perhaps it's a matter of survival, and if they went to a childminder, it would provide socialising for them, and three hours is hardly farming out.'

He arrived home in time to put the children in the bath and get them ready for their cots, and although he knew they could not understand a word he was saying, he loved to read them a story and they loved to hear it read. Tonight it was Peppa Pig which they recognised from the DVD they sometimes were allowed to watch. Mummy then fed them (which daddy certainly couldn't manage though he loved to watch) and daddy carried them both upstairs to their room. Chloe normally fell asleep more or less at once but George took a little longer and made all sorts of singing noises, and then all became quiet.

As yet Emily and Alex had not had the chance to say even a few words to each other so engrossed were they in the children, but in the kitchen as they prepared supper there was every opportunity to speak. Alex recounted his conversation with Amy including the possibility of a childminder or nanny.

'I suppose we've been really lucky so far,' said Emily, 'that mum's been able to do as much as she has whilst George and Chloe have been really small. But she's quite right, she's getting older and if the twins exhaust us, how much more will that be the case for her and more during the next year when they become mobile?'

'I said to her that I wasn't prepared to countenance anything that would get in the way of your work. That is always the priority nor would I want the children to grow up thinking they weren't loved and cared for because we put our own work needs before them.'

Emily came to Alex and put her arms round his shoulders and said:

'How do I love thee? Let me count the ways.
  I love thee to the depth and breadth and height
  My soul can reach, when feeling out of sight
  For the ends of being and ideal grace.
  I love thee to the level of every day's
  Most quiet need, by sun and candle-light.
  I love thee freely, as men strive for right.
  I love thee purely, as they turn from praise.
  I love thee with the passion put to use
  In my old griefs, and with my childhood's faith.
  I love thee with a love I seemed to lose
  With my lost saints. I love thee with the breath,
  Smiles, tears, of all my life; and, if God choose,
  I shall but love thee better after death.'

She kissed him.

'We won't worry too much about the final line, but Elizabeth Barrett Browning could just as easily be speaking for me, as for her own love for Robert.'

Alex now had tears running down his face.

'It's not unusual for children to go to a childminder, or to have someone come and look after them at home, and I imagine that before too long we'll be looking for a nursery for them anyway. Those things are quite usual and from what I've seen the children in them very much enjoy being there with others. I'm not sure a nanny is a good idea because once the children are walking they will always want to come and interrupt us and, knowing us, we'll be delighted for them to do so. I'm not sure how we set about seeking a childminder – perhaps you have contacts through your National Park group that could help us.'

'Well, I have a meeting next week and I'll mention it.'

The phone rang and standing next to it, Emily answered. She handed it to Alex.

'Hello. Alex Elliot here.'

'Hello Mr Elliot. You don't know me though I'm very much hoping we can meet soon. My name is Tom Kiernan. I've received a letter from the Cabinet Office saying that you are a member of the Parole Board who will make decisions about whether Theodore Armstrong, the bastard who killed my daughters, will be granted parole in the light of his application. The letter says you will be coming to see me. Is that right?'

'Yes it is, but I'm not actually a member of the Parole Board. My job is to be an independent liaison between all those involved and my recommendation will be taken into consideration when the Board meets. You will have the opportunity, if you so wish, to make a statement, or to have a statement read by another on your behalf, whether in the presence of Armstrong or not – all of this will be your decision. I very much want to come and meet you and hear from you in person what you feel about the application.

'As I'm sure you know, Armstrong has been sentenced to life

imprisonment and the judge indicated that he should not be liable for parole until at least 20 years have passed. But I'm not at all convinced that your pain will have diminished one little bit in that time and that should receive the greatest consideration when the Board meets.'

'Thank you for that, sir. I don't of course know where you live but when might you be able to come?'

'The sooner the better. Would you be willing for me to telephone you back before nine o'clock in the morning so that we can agree on a time and day? I can't do it just at this moment.'

'Of course, sir. Shall I give you my phone number?'

'No need, this phone records all incoming numbers. I will also need to speak to your former wife who lives in Penrith. She also will have heard from the Parole Board.'

'The break-up of our marriage is another casualty of what Armstrong did. Do you know where Pooley Bridge is?'

'Fortunately my sat-nav does. We'll speak before 9 o'clock. Will that suit you?'

'Yes. Good night, sir.'

Alex put the phone down.

'That poor man. But I've had an idea. How would you fancy a trip to the Lake District, all of us? If you could cope with the kids while I go to see Mr Kiernan and the former Mrs Kiernan, now Mrs Gathercole, the rest of the time will be ours.'

'That would be wonderful.'

After supper Alex telephoned the secretary of the National Park to see if she knew where they might look for a childminder. It turned out that her daughter was a licensed childminder and had recently received a glowing report from Ofsted. She gave Alex her number and said she was sure she would be able to fit Chloe and George in.

'Thank you, I'll give her a ring tonight if I may and see what she has to say.'

'Will you be at the meeting on Monday morning, Alex.'

'I'm afraid so, but if it's anything like last time it will be my last meeting. You and I in particular don't have to put up with that pile of excrement.'

'In which case I will attend too, but I really don't want to do so. If I want a gathering of children then I'll visit my daughter when she's got all her children there.'

'The thing is, I have another reason for wanting to resign. I've been asked to take on a special job by the Cabinet Office relating to prisons, which will be good practice for when they lock me up in one. It's going to be quite demanding so keep this under your hat until then, but the chances are that Monday will be my final meeting.'

'In which case, Alex, it will also be mine. I've only gone on to support you.'

'Thank you for that and now I'll get Emily to call Fiona, as these things are best talked over by women.'

'I'll take that from you but I wouldn't take it from anyone else. See you on Monday.'

Whilst Alex had been on the house phone, Emily had called her mother on her mobile expressing the hope that she would like to come to the Lake District with them in the following week. She was delighted. Now, Emily turned to her computer and began the task of finding somewhere for them to stay wouldn't be easy with two small children and a granny in tow. She broke off to telephone Fiona to begin making arrangements for the twins to go to her for three hours each weekday morning beginning the week after next. She then returned to the Internet and more than an hour later called out "Success!". It was a cottage in a place called Glenridding which looked and sounded good. There had been a cancellation so the owner was delighted too.

It was just after 8:45 when Alex telephoned Pooley Bridge, and it was answered by Mr Kiernan.

'True to your word – thank you Mr Elliot. Believe me it hasn't always been like that so it bodes well for our meeting.'

'My family are coming up with me and we've arranged to stay close by so we won't be far from where you are. I am entirely at your disposal but would happily come and see you on Tuesday morning if that suited you.'

'Yes, Tuesday morning will be fine. What time have you in mind?'

'Shall we say 10 o'clock?'

'That will be fine.'

'Let me give you my mobile number so that if anything changes, anything at all, you can let me know and we'll re-arrange.'

Alex then called Mattie Gathercole who had been expecting a call as she had been forewarned by Tom Kiernan. She agreed to a meeting at 11-30.

Chapter Six

When the request had first come to be the chair of the Peak District National Park Trustees Committee, Alex was surprised to say the least, as he had no expertise to offer on the subject of how to run a national park, but after a few meetings he began to realise that he was expected to bring a different expertise to the task. Those appointing him had assumed that as a former philosopher and bishop he was bound to have the calming influence on those members of the committee known to be highly irascible. Alex and the committee secretary, Christine, often looked at one another in total exasperation whilst the others shouted at each other. At the last meeting she had been astonished to see that whilst the normal arguments were taking place, the chairman had produced a book out of his bag which he sat there reading.

The Monday morning meeting in Buxton unfortunately took the same form, and arguments began almost as soon as they arrived. There were two trustees on either side who were the main protagonists but others joined in and it often became very noisy. Alex banged the table and smiled.

'Well, I think we're all in agreement about that. So we come to the next item on the agenda, well it's not on the agenda as such, but I am exercising my prerogative as chairman to put it there. It is to let you know that I am here and now resigning my position, and I very much hope you will all grow up and stop playing silly buggers when my successor is appointed.'

'I am resigning of this moment also,' added Christine.

Before anyone could speak and in the meeting there was a rare silence, Alex and Fiona stood, put their papers into their files, wished everyone a good morning, and left.

'I rather like Buxton,' said Alex. 'Is there anywhere we can get a good cup of coffee?'

'Follow me.'

They walked down the road towards the centre of town, laughing as they did so, feeling very much like children at the end of term. The coffee shop was not one of the modern American or Continental style shops, but a very English looking place, though it turned out that the coffee was superb and they both gave in, as a way of celebration, to toasted teacakes.

'Am I allowed to know a little more of this new job you have?' asked Christine.

'I'm a sort of adviser on parole in a particular prison. Whether my observations and comments will have any influence on the work of the Parole Board as they make their decisions I don't know, but I assume that having appointed me there is some reason for it.'

'I don't think I'd like to go into a prison though all I know is what I see sometimes on the news and they don't give the appearance of being very nice places and have a lot of trouble with drugs being smuggled in or even flown in by drone, and they seem pretty violent places.'

'Some of them are all those things, and the government struggles to know what to do about them. The prison population is huge, though fortunately I only visit a relatively small institution.'

'What about victims? This seems to me that all too easily they are overlooked and all the attention seems to be given to the needs of those who committed the crimes.'

'If I wore one, I would raise my hat every time to those who work in them. They get endlessly provoked and need the patience of Job.'

'It sounds to me that it's not totally unlike the committee we've both just resigned from!'

Alex laughed.

'Tell me about Fiona.'

'She pretty bright and left school with good A-levels, but not quite bright enough to say No, so by the time she was 20 she already had a child of her own, but no man to go with it, but she is very resourceful and decided she wanted to work with children so she decided to train as a nursery nurse, and after she got married and had two more children realised that she could combine her own need of childcare with those of others and became a registered childminder. She does love children which, I suppose is essential, but she's recently had an OFSTED inspection and they were very impressed. So your twins will enjoy themselves and it will be a good multiracial experience for them.'

'Is she intending to have any more herself?'

'Oh no.'

'And her husband?'

'Tim works at the opera house. He's smashing and a great dad as well as a great husband, and he's chosen well because, though I say it myself, Fiona is quite a looker.'

'Well, Emily and I are hugely grateful to you both.'

'And what about you and your wife. Are you hoping for more children?'

'If we are I can only hope they're not twins this time!'

After lunch, with the car packed, they set off for the Lake

District, with Emily driving the car. She was used to making this journey because in the days when she was on the reading circuit, she did so in places such as Kendal and Keswick, which she loved going to because the surrounding countryside was so wonderful. The journey via the M6 took just three and a half hours, which included stops for baby feeding and changing, and food for mummy, daddy and granny to save having to cook on arrival. It was a lovely sunny evening and as they drove along the lakeside they were almost overwhelmed by the beauty of Ullswater and its surrounding hills. It was such a good place to visit. The twins of course had the priority when it came to unloading and Amy and Alex each made up a cot whilst Emily heated up something from a bottle which they both obviously enjoyed and once nappies were changed and pyjamas put on, she fed them, though both of them looked as if they knew they were missing a bath. Having slept most of the way, however, they were not particularly minded to sleep now so the adults took it in turn to eat and then go to the children. It was about 10 o'clock when George finally went off, Chloe having beaten him by about 10 minutes.

Between cot visits, Alex had once again looked over the papers pertaining to the murders of the two Kiernan girls, one eight and the other six. It truly was a horror story, and he wasn't looking forward to meeting Mr Kiernan and Mrs Gathercole in the morning, and he thought back to his conversation with Amy of the previous week. Certainly he could do with some sort of compass and sextant as he met with them.

Both children ended up in their parents' bed for having woken up in a strange place they instantly became restless and called out. Alex had Chloe immediately next to him in the bed and looking at her, wondered how he would cope if the same thing that happened to the Kiernan girls happened to her. He knew himself well enough to know that there could be no turning of the other cheek and that what he would want was revenge. In the past he had not given a great deal of thought to capital punishment as it had been abolished well before his time, though he knew that if there ever was a referendum on the subject, the British people would bring it back at the first opportunity. Its abolition raised the problem he was going to face this morning which was how do you do justice to such a heinous crime? Armstrong was looking for another chance to live normally, a second chance, and if it was judged that he was no longer a danger to anyone, could it possibly be right to keep him in prison? He presented well but therein lay the real difficulty – was it nothing but presentation?

Over breakfast, Emily and Amy said they would like to take the twins along the lakeside and when Alex returned, they would be handed over to him, as mother and daughter were intending to drive over the Kirkstone Pass to do some shopping at *Booths* supermarket in Windermere. Alex smiled his approval, but already he was planning in his mind how he might hijack being abandoned in this way and ensure that he and the children would also get to Windermere.

Pooley Bridge was not far away, and he easily found the road in which Tom Kiernan lived, and then the house, parking outside. Deliberately he was carrying no file or any other sign of paperwork though he had to remember that this was not a pastoral visit, the sort of thing he had been used to doing as a priest, but something quite different for which the government was paying him and expecting him to give of his best. The door was opened before he got there. Mr Kiernan was tall and rather gaunt and such hair as he still had was grey. Once inside Alex's attention was immediately drawn to a photograph of two girls he supposed to be Anna and Rose. Mr Kiernan noticed where his attention was being given.

'That's Anna on the left and Rose on the right. They favoured one another and were extremely close and died together.'

'Are you intending to make a statement when the Parole Board meets?'

'Definitely, though as yet I haven't decided whether or not I want Armstrong present.'

'Well you probably have a little more time to make that decision. A Parole Board takes about six months, as I'm sure you've been told, to prepare everything and of course at any one time there are a lot of people in prison applying for parole.'

'It was the same with the trial. It took ages.'

'I have two small children and I cannot imagine for one moment what it must have been like for you to go through that experience. People sometimes use the word harrowing, but it must have been far worse.'

'It was,' said Mr Kiernan. 'And as I sat there listening to the pathologist I think it was, describing in detail what had happened to Anna and Rose, I thought to myself how can I kill this man? Until that moment I'd never been in favour of capital punishment but I can tell you Mr Elliot, I would quite happily have put the noose round his neck and let him drop.'

'I certainly don't blame you for that and I honestly think every parent would sympathise with you. When I look at that photograph I wonder how on earth I'm going to be able to be in control of myself when I have next to sit in a room with Armstrong.'

'Have you met him yet?' asked Mr Kiernan.

'I did so last week in Banklyn.'

'Did he mention what he did to Anna and Rose?'

'I hope you'll understand, but I'm not at liberty to report anything he said or did not say as it may be part of his appeal to the Board, but because I'm a parent myself, I would very much like you to tell me about Anna and Rose if you feel able to do so.

Despite what Armstrong did, they are still your children, still those you love greatly.'

Mr Kiernan began to speak, though said little before the tears came. Alex found it almost unbearable.

'I have to say Mr Elliot, I was dreading your coming today because I assumed you'd be like the lawyers we dealt with – you know, just doing their cold duty, but it hasn't felt like that, I'm pleased to say. There's a cheeky question I'd like to ask. I went on the Internet to see if I could find anything about you. The nearest I could get was someone with your name who'd been a professor and a bishop. When you arrived, and I saw how young you were I realised that it couldn't possibly be you, or could it?'

'I was both of those things but now I'm neither. For most of the time I'm just daddy and husband and son-in-law. They are the best titles I've ever had and I want no more.'

'I've never been particularly religious, but going through what we went through is difficult to square with what a lot of religious people come out with.'

'What happened to your girls cannot possibly be made sense of. I no longer practice any religion, other than my attempts at loving people.'

'That's a real worthy aim to live by and bring your children up with, but you might understand that I can't manage any sort of love or forgiveness towards the man who destroyed my daughters so wickedly.'

Alex stood.

'Before I leave, I have to point out that I'm not able to tell you what my report on my visit to see you will contain, but if I were you, I really wouldn't lose any sleep over it, if you take my meaning'

'Thank you.'

For some reason which almost certainly had to do with the way in which Alex had set it, the sat-nav now more or less refused to play ball. Fortunately it was not very far up the road to Penrith and once there he was able to find his way even without technology.

The house, outside which he parked, suggested that Mrs Gathercole had done rather better for herself in her second marriage than in her first and when she opened the front door to him, she didn't have the same pain written over her face that he had seen on her former husband though he could see how well made-up she was. There was no sign of the new husband, nor were there photographs of Anna or Rose but he did catch sight of one he took to be of a ten-year-old boy.

'That's our son, Eric,' she said, seeing where he was looking. 'There are no photographs of Anna or Rose on show because I don't think that would be at all fair on my husband, but of course I have plenty and there's hardly a day goes by when I don't look at them. The chances are they would have families of their own by now but it wasn't to be. I loved and adored them and will never be able to forgive myself for allowing them to be outside where that monster was biding his time. Now Mr Elliot, let's have a cup of tea.'

'Thank you Mrs Gathercole,' said Alex even if it was the last thing in the world he wanted.

'Please call me Mattie.'

'Thank you, I will and I'm Alex.'

Whilst she was away Alex looked round the room more closely. Whatever work her husband was engaged in, they seemed to have enough money to have good things around them, and the television screen was probably the largest Alex had ever seen.

'Milk and sugar?' as Mattie returned to the room.

'Just a little milk please.'

Once they had settled Alex thought he ought to take the

initiative.

'As I'm sure you have been informed by the Parole Board, Theodore Armstrong, having completed the minimum sentence given by the judge at his trial, has applied for parole, as is his right under the law, no matter what we might feel about that that. Lots of people, lots of the time, are given parole, mostly I think to keep the prison population as low as possible though it is proving difficult to do so. Some people in prison will remain there for the rest of their lives, and others, such as Armstrong, can ask to be considered for release under licence after their minimum term has been completed.

'Armstrong was given a life sentence, not a sentence of 20 years, and I'm sure you will remember only too well the judge saying that he would not be considered for parole until at least 20 years had passed. In the case of someone who has committed such terrible acts, all the resources of the Parole Board are brought to bear in consideration of the application. I am one of those resources. My job is to liaise between all parties involved beginning with you and your former husband, with the prison staff who see him on a day-to-day basis, with those who make a psychiatric or psychological assessment, with at least one judge and other legal experts, and also of course, the prisoner himself. Each of us contributes to the process of assessment, and of course that includes your own participation when the Board meets if you wish.

'I imagine that all this is familiar to you. I met Armstrong for the first time last week in Banklyn prison and I shall do so again. But my purpose today is to listen to you.'

'We knew Teddy Armstrong around the village and people were always very suspicious of him. There was always something you felt you couldn't trust in him. Perhaps you'll think it's not relevant, but he had a reputation for hanging around the bus stop in the afternoon waiting for the girls coming home from school. As far as I know he never had any actual physical contact with them but he looked at them in a way that I always thought suspicious when I saw him. He was a loner, quite intelligent I think, and at the time the police said there were a lot of books in his house. He went on to the Parish Council for a year when a woman took a maternity break. Apparently he didn't say a great deal and as it was only a casual vacancy, that was probably right, but the Chairman of the Council did say to me once that he'd noticed that when there was something being discussed that he was interested in, Armstrong became highly manipulative, even to the extent of implying that he knew certain things about members which perhaps ought to see the light of day if he didn't get his way. They were ever so glad to be shot of him at the end of the year.

'Tom always tried to make sure the girls kept well away from him and would never let them out if he knew he was around. Pooley Bridge is a small place so Armstrong stood out. There was a cretin who called himself the vicar who sought to befriend him. He was as bad a judge of character as he was a man of the cloth. Believe it or not, he had an affair with one of his churchwardens and unsurprisingly his wife left him and he then moved the churchwarden into the vicarage with him and began proceedings for a divorce. I think the church should have thrown him out. It was a disgrace, but would you believe it, the Bishop of Carlisle offered him another job!

'Tom had gone out fishing, and Anna and Rose were inside with me and wanted to go out to play because it was a sunny evening, so I let them. About an hour later Tom came back and asked where the girls were. We both went out to look, expecting them to find them in one of their usual places for play. They were very close even though there were two years between them and loved to play together rather than with other kids. When we weren't able to find them we started to panic, and I went back home to phone the police whilst Tom kept on looking. At first the police just sent one man, but he soon realised that something was up and before long the place was running with police. They did a house-to-house search and when they got to Armstrong's house there was no reply though, when one of his neighbours expressed concern about strange noises they'd heard a little earlier, the police broke his door down. He was sitting calmly in an armchair watching the tele, and upstairs they found Anna and Rose.'

Alex and Mattie sat in silence for some time.

'Did you see the bodies of your children?'

'They advised us not to and when I heard all that the pathologist said at the trial, I was glad to have taken that advice. By all accounts it was terrible.'

'I can't begin to imagine the effect this has had upon your life, Mattie. After all, we are talking about something that is best described as evil, and would you say that one of its effects was the breakdown of your marriage to Tom?'

'At first we tried all we could to support one another, and the local community was terrific. But after a while, and I'm really not blaming him for this, Tom started drinking. He'd always had a drink but always knew when to stop. Up to that time I had never seen him drunk, and he never drank in front of the children. Now he was drinking heavily most of the time, often beginning in the morning. You can make excuses for people, Alex, in particular circumstances and God only knows ours were very particular, but nothing could excuse his badly treating me, hitting me and leaving obvious bruises on my face and trying to force himself upon me. That was when I realised our marriage was over and one day, when he was out, I left and moved in with my closest friend Maureen in Penrith. She encouraged me to try my best at living again. Maureen is the salt of the earth and her philosophy is very much bound up with picking yourself up, dusting yourself off, and starting all over again. It wasn't easy I can tell you. One day Maureen got tickets for the cinema at the Rheged Centre on the Keswick Road. We went for some food first and sat at a table where we got chatting with Barney, who had been widowed quite young. That's how it all began and I am so lucky to have found him, but it's no use asking me what the film was because I just can't remember.'

'What do you think should be done in response to Armstrong's application for parole?'

'It wouldn't surprise me from what we knew of him before this happened if he is able to present himself positively and full of sorrow for what he has done and making clear his determination never to do the same again so that he is no harm to anyone. Obviously you've met him and the reality may be totally different from that, but as my friend Maureen says, leopards really don't change their spots. For what he did to my lovely girls, and what he does to this day to Tom and me, bringing about our divorce, even if I at least have been luckier than Tom, my own feeling is that he should never leave the prison.'

'Thank you Mattie for being so candid in all that you have told me. I'm sure you will understand that I'm not able to tell you what will be in my report, just as I can't tell you anything about Armstrong and what I shall have to say about him. I very much hope you will accept the invitation to the Board. Whether you have Armstrong in the room when you speak is entirely up to you, but I feel you should exercise your right to make a statement.'

As he made his way back to Glenridding, this time with the sat-nav working again, it struck Alex that one of the key issues he needed to consider was the matter of truth and who was telling it. Tom Kiernan had been considerably less forthcoming than his former wife, but had she been telling him what she wanted him to think? On the other hand he was struck by her memory of Armstrong as someone who put on a front and he really had no honest reason to doubt what she was saying. The events of two decades ago were seared into their minds and bodies. Tom had clearly been destroyed but Mattie had, not least through the help of her friend Maureen, managed some sort of life. The letters to Armstrong shown to him by the prison authorities had almost certainly come from Tom though Alex had not asked him outright. If Armstrong were to be released and given a new identity, Alex thought Tom might move heaven and earth to find him, however difficult it might prove, and possibly kill him. As he drove along the side of Ullswater, Alex thought that he might well do the same himself which was a chilling thought and the sort he would never have imagined himself having. Change the name of the children to Chloe and George, and he knew why.

Chapter Seven

In the high chairs kindly provided for them by the owner, the children express their delight on the arrival of daddy by disposing of most of their food onto the floor. It was an renewing experience to be back with the family though both Emily and Amy could see that the morning had been demanding. So it was they who decided that Alex should come with them to Windermere and not be left alone with the children. Alex ate a sandwich, helped clear the floor and did the washing up, the kind of tasks which he hoped would neutralise his morning. Then they got ready, loaded the children into the car and set off, Amy driving up the Kirkstone Pass. It was a sunny day and they could see for miles, though Chloe and George could see nothing, their eyes being closed in sleep. And then they began the descent into the lakeside town of Windermere which boasts one of the finest supermarkets in the world: *Booth's,* a company found only in the North-West. The car park was almost completely full but Amy found a space, and then the five of them set off into the store to equip them with food for the remainder of the week.

Once their trolley was full, Alex walked it back to the car and emptied it into the boot, then returning to the others who by now were on the opposite side of the store looking at the railway station from where the line ran to distant Manchester airport. The line did not continue the other way on to Ambleside and Grasmere because Wordsworth had said No! He didn't want tourists anywhere near him, but of course he hadn't foreseen the arrival of the internal combustion engine. More important than the railway station however, was what stood just 50 yards further on: the headquarters of *Lakeland* and within it the most marvellous café and restaurant on the first floor which with a pushchair they had to enter via the lift but which offered the most marvellous views from the enormous curved windows.

After his sandwich lunch, Alex was ready for something more substantial and chose a Ciabatta with Lancashire cheese and tomato pickle, whilst Emily and Amy each had a piece of Lemon Drizzle Cake, some of which they fed to the twins, all washed down with Lakeland Blend tea.

'It must be a great disappointment to you,' said Alex, 'that you felt you had to bring me with you because I'm pretty sure if you had come without me, you would have had one of their full meals.'

'That's a scandalous accusation,' said Emily. 'I am deeply shocked that you could think such a thing of your wife and mother-in-law. I'm tempted to make you walk all the way back.'

'Pushing the buggy with the twins in as well, no doubt.'

'No, just the empty buggy. I'm surprised you think I'm that terrible.'

'Oh I do, I do. I can never forget what you did to me in America when you made me change my life forever. How could I ever trust you after that?'

'You're right and I pretty much think about it every single day.'

'Me too, and will there ever be a poem about it, I wonder?'

'Yes, I've wondered that too,' said Amy, who was quite used to silly banter between them.

'It's most odd but every time I try, I just can't continue, so I concluded that the time is not yet right but I do hope it will come, as I want it for Chloe and George, so they know.'

Amy looked over at Alex.

'I suppose the fact that you've not told us anything at all about the morning indicates that you're not allowed to do so.'

'I'm certainly not allowed to show anyone the content of my report to the Parole Board but I'm quite some time away from that. As for the morning, it was about as painful as you might imagine. Two lives and two people who will never recover from what happened. They are now divorced though I gather that's not entirely unusual in such circumstances, and she is making a go at life, and has even had another child with her new husband but the prisoner in Banklyn not only committed sacrilege, he has also left behind him a perpetual memory of the hell into which they entered.

'I have of course, as both of you have, read about such things in the newspaper or on the television news and just for a moment we find ourselves taken aback, but then the news moves on to something else and in a very short time we have forgotten all about it. Those parents have not and cannot.'

There was silence for a little while.

'Do you know what?' said Emily, ' I think we should drive down to Bowness and feed the ducks on the lake.'

It was inevitable that it would happen one day. That it should happen here in the Lake District was not at all predictable, but as Alex made his way pushing the buggy out towards the exit, a familiar face stopped in front of him.

'Father,' said a young man, 'it's wonderful to see you here and if that lady with you is the reason you retired from the diocese, then it's hardly surprising, if you and she don't mind me saying so.'

The young man was accompanied by another young man, but not one that Alex recognised.

'Peter, it's so good to see you. How are you doing and are you surviving under my old friend Colin?'

'Most of us knew him anyway and were delighted when he was appointed as your successor but I'm sure you know you are greatly missed and I personally feel even my own ministry is the less without you there as my bishop, not least the fact that you ordained me.'

'I'm proud to have done so and I don't forget any of those it was my privilege and responsibility to ordain and you uppermost among them.'

'Did I cause you a lot of hassle?'

'Not at all. I knew you were going to be a very fine priest and the question of who you went to bed with was a matter neither for me nor anyone else. But you haven't introduced me to your companion.'

'Huby, this is Bishop Alex, Bishop Alex this is Huby.'

'It's a new name on me,' said Alex.

'My parents were born towards the end of the eighteenth century,' said Huby, 'and therefore gave me the name Hubert.'

'Oh my God, that's awful,' said Emily.

'So I decided to repay them by being gay.'

They all laughed together.

'Well Father, I mustn't delay you and your family, but seeing you today has meant a great deal to me. The loss to the church by your departure is considerable. I wish you much happiness and if these two children are yours, then they at least can grow up happy in the knowledge that they look considerably more like their mother than their father.'

'I can't disagree. Here is a card with our address and email on it. Please be in touch, Peter, and come and stay, and not necessarily alone.'

Alex pulled out a card from his pocket and handed it over. Peter nodded, deeply moved. They continued out through the exit and turned right down towards the supermarket once more.

'It's obvious what he was but who was he?'

'He's called Peter Cheeseman and of those I ordained in Truro he was by far and away the best. Academically he wasn't anything special, but in terms of being a person of commitment he stood out. He also has a wonderful sense of humour as you saw. As you will have gathered he's gay, and before his ordination came to see me and told me all about it, and I thanked him but said I wasn't interested in his sexual life which I was sure he exercised responsibly, as I would have said to any priest whether straight or gay. It was at the same time the House of Bishops was being dragooned by the Archbishop into producing a list to be kept at Lambeth of gay and lesbian clergy. I argued against it and continued to do so as we sat together in a sanctimonious huddle when we met. Eventually his nibs looking straight at me said this had to be agreed by us all if it was going to happen, and many of the other evangelicals (or the brain dead, as I thought of them) also joined him in his accusatory stare. I said that he was quite right to say it would only work if every one of signed up for it, because without my vote I was pleased to know it would fail. He still insisted we vote by a show of hands, hoping perhaps to shame me and was suitably rewarded, to my delight, with three hands of dissent. I don't think he liked me from that day on. So Peter Cheeseman's name would not be added to any list.'

'I noticed you didn't invite Huby.'

'That's because I have no idea who he is. He may be Peter's partner or he may be someone he met earlier in the day. Peter will understand that, just as I have to apologise to Amy that Peter didn't say how beautiful you are too.'

'I'll survive, Father, but I'm proud of you', Amy replied with a huge smile.

Bowness was busy as usual. They fed the ducks which Chloe and George adored. They would quite like to have taken them to the Beatrix Potter Museum but decided, after a little discussion, that a year from now would be a better time to introduce them to the world of Peter Rabbit, and that it might actually frighten them a little now and turn them off the stories when the time came for them to hear them.

'Beatrix Potter has long been one of my heroes, 'said Amy. 'Emily's father and I used to love reading the stories to her, but so entranced was I by them, that I began doing some research into her life. I was therefore appalled when the film *Miss Potter* came out. In the first place because they had an American, Reneée Zellweger who'd played Bridget Jones earlier, as Beatrix, but what was far worse was the way in which they trivialised absolutely everything, but especially Beatrix herself. She was in fact a tough woman who gave her life to supporting farming communities in Cumberland, as it was, maintaining the standard of Herdwick sheep which she often judged at shows. But playing her as something corny was quite unforgivable and aren't there any English actresses who could have played the part? I never bought the DVD, as you might well imagine.'

'Trivialising and sentimentalising has become standard fare I'm afraid,' added Emily. 'I've always striven to avoid it in my poetry but that's where we are as a people.'

For supper Amy made sausages and mash which they tucked into after the children were asleep.

'What struck me most this morning,' said Alex, 'is that in both instances I parked my car outside and then entered houses that were perfectly normal from outside, with nothing to distinguish them in any way, but behind the front door there was a different reality altogether, in the first truly a house of horrors, the second not quite as much because the mother remarried and had another baby, but she is profoundly scarred by it all.'

'That quite true,' said Amy, 'and I have often thought it as I've wandered around the Meadowhall Centre in Sheffield seeing people shopping and I've wondered what lies behind their faces, what private heavens and what private hells. I've never been into a prison but I daresay, Alex, one of the things you will have to face up to is that even those who have done the very worst things imaginable to others, don't have the word evil stamped onto their foreheads. They look just like we do.'

'I once met a Labour MP,' said Alex, 'a former miner, as rough and ready as they come who told me that he had often found that to be the case. People would sit in his surgery and as he looked at them he wondered why on earth they were there as they looked so perfectly normal, but when their turn came to speak to him it was often very different. Em, who was it who wrote: "The mass of men lead lives of quiet desperation."?'

'Thoreau,' she replied.

Alex turned to Amy.

'Did you know what a clever daughter you produced, Mrs Cunningham?'

'She was clever enough to marry you.'

'And I can tell you that if she were not here and could hear me, I would say to you that I adore her more and more each day.'

For the rest of the week Alex was able to put out of his mind completely the parents of Anna and Rose. Fell walking was completely out of the question even though Amy offered to look after the children to allow Emily and Alex the opportunity but they decided against. Walking here was tough and demanding and always exhausting, but they went out for walks together where they could see great beauty. Emily told Alex the story of how the Wordsworths came to live in Grasmere and although she loved much of the poetry of William, she concentrated her narrative on his sister, Dorothy, who, she said, in the past 30 also years, has been rediscovered by feminist literary critics and historians. That was the moment they decided that on the following morning they would all go over the Kirkstone Pass again and visit Rydal and Grasmere.

On the following morning Amy said she would quite like a day off and spend it reading, so it was just two parents and two children who made their way up and over the hill and instead of turning left to Windermere, they turned right and soon passed through Ambleside before coming to Rydal Water and turning left into Grasmere and the large car park on the right.

'There will be a lot of people here later,' said Emily, 'so it might be sensible to go and visit the Wordsworth Museum first.'

Chloe travelled across the road to the museum on the back of her father, George on his mother. Neither were quite old enough to be able to take advantage of the special children's area in the Centre, but there would be other days. They went into Dove Cottage and then asked to be admitted to the new Library in the Jerwood Centre. There was a moment's hesitation because of the presence of the children, but Emily reassured them that the chances of the children getting anywhere near an exhibit or a book was nil. Whether this would have worked was soon a redundant matter, because one of the staff recognised Emily and had attended a number of her readings and owned some of her books. She did better than just letting them in, she gave them a guided tour which they hugely enjoyed. The news that a significant poet was on the premises spread quickly and soon they were joined by the Director of the Jerwood Centre.

'A very warm welcome Ms Cunningham. It's a great honour for us to have you here and before you leave, please make sure you sign some copies of your books in the shop.'

'Thank you, this is my husband, Alex, and we bear on our backs our twins Chloe and George'

'Have you been before?'

'I have but it's always such a pleasure to return.'

'Which is almost exactly what Wordsworth said whenever he returned from a journey.'

'I think Rebecca Watts worked here for a while. She's a brilliant poet.'

'She did and has written a fine poem about here, which I suspect you know.'

'Oh yes. It's outstanding.'

The Director showed them various treasures. and both Emily and Alex thought his enthusiasm a positive gift to the place and its visitors and students. Eventually after the signings and conversations with customers and staff they left the Centre and made their way across the road and into Grasmere, where Emily was almost as desperate to feed them as the twins were to suckle. 'I think weaning time has come,' she said, as they sat in the Garden Village with their coffees, onlookers amazed by the sight of her breast feeding two at the same time.

Chapter Eight

Linda and Andy Wilson lived in a large house in the village of Long Riston, a few miles to the east of Beverley. For a village it was sometimes busy but on the edge of beautiful countryside in which Linda liked to walk. She would have quite liked a dog but Andy didn't care for them so mostly her walks were taken alone. She was in her early 50's and felt she was still attractive, even if her husband was no longer especially attentive on the bedroom front.

Andy stopped at the Bluebell, Old Ellerby, each evening on his way home from work for an unwinding pint. One evening two men, one older than the other, began chatting with him.

'What's it like working in a prison?' the younger one asked Andy.

'How would I know?'

'My son did six months for VAT fraud,' said the older man. 'But being in self-employment is always risky especially these days, though you don't need me to tell you that. I'm sure Karl tells you how bad things are. He's in real financial difficulties but I'm sure, as his dad, you know all about it.'

Andy stood.

'I should be getting off home.'

'Do sit down Andy and think sensibly about Karl and how you

can perhaps help him save his business, not least on the basis of five grand as a good-will starter, followed by two grand a month thereafter.'

Andy said nothing.

'You see Andy, we do our research properly. Not only do we know about the state of your son's business and the serious difficulties with his mortgage, we also know that there are two people only who enter Banklyn each day without a search or the attention of sniffer dogs, and that's you and your deputy Myles Hammond. What we are suggesting is simple and straightforward, which is that once a week you take a different briefcase with you into work and make sure you leave it alone for no more than ten minutes in your office. Easy-peasy. It looks just like your normal case. Anything more you don't need to know and it's probably best that you don't. We're not going to pressure you Andy and you'll probably want to talk it over with your wife, and possibly your son too. There's no question that Karl's business would be not just helped but actually saved by a regular injection of funds and your two grandchildren might still have somewhere to live.'

Andy told Linda about this as soon as he reached home, and at once decided to call the police and a special number he had for the Ministry of Justice but decided to have supper before making the calls. Linda noticed the hesitation and delay.

'And how would you being in prison for smuggling what we must assume to be drugs into Banklyn help Karl, or me for that matter?' asked Linda, angry and concerned.

'As they explained it to me, the system is more or less foolproof.'

'Most people inside have no doubt thought precisely that at some time or other and look where they are now. You are risking everything, including your pension. I can't possibly agree to it, and if you go ahead I shall feel duty bound to let the police know. You can't do this. It's so incredibly stupid and contrary to all that you've ever claimed to believe in. You are a senior prison governor, for Christ's sake.'

'And our son's business is on the verge of collapse and he may well be about to lose his house. Are you willing to let him know that we could have saved his business and his house, and that includes Joan and our two grandchildren, but that we chose not to do so.'

'Andy, if you go ahead with this, I shall leave you and get a divorce, and all the money from the settlement I will give to Karl and Joan, which will more than keep them in business and in their home, and please don't for one moment think that I'm joking, because I'm not.'

She stood at the table and then stormed out. Andy sat there surveying the food largely not eaten and thought about it all. There was in it an element he had not mentioned to her, and it was that he was bored. Some might call it a midlife crisis but more than anything he knew he was just bored. He had been doing this for more than 25 years, picking up society's shit on a daily basis. Whether what had been suggested to him could bring him a measure of excitement otherwise lacking in his life, he didn't and couldn't know, but it might. And then he found himself wondering just what he was thinking. This was criminal activity of an extreme kind and Linda was quite right, he would be unbelievably stupid to countenance it.

He cleared the table and loaded the dishwasher before going through to the lounge where he found Linda on the phone to Karl.

'How much?' were the first words he heard her say.

'Karl, why the hell haven't you told us this before? And how long before you lose your house?'

As he listened, Andy knew that what he had been told earlier by the two men was true.

'Does Joan know all about this? So, what were you intending to do? Of course you could come and live here, but that would mean the total collapse of the business, the loss of Joan's job and changing schools for the children. Look, Karl, there's a possibility that we might be able to help you very soon in the form of an injection of capital, a sort of lump-sum and then monthly contributions. Oh you mustn't worry about that. Just take it from me that we wouldn't do it if we couldn't. Give me a couple of days and I'll be able to give you facts and figures. Yes he's sitting with me now and I'm pretty certain he's totally in support of all I'm saying, and in fact he's nodding his head, though he could be falling asleep! Please give our love to Joan and the children. Bye.'

She put the phone down. 'How on earth did they find all this out about the business and the mortgage? Because they've got it exactly right. He's in big trouble with the bank and the building society and both are threatening to foreclose in a matter of weeks.'

'Did he say anything at all about how it has happened?'

'Oh just the usual things that happen to businesses all the time, though you and I both know that he's quite capable of making bad decisions by not thinking things through.'

'Precisely what I am doing.'

Two evenings later, Andy pulled into the car park of the pub, waited a little while to see if he was being followed and then dismissed the idea as pure paranoia. He went into the bar and ordered his usual pint. Out of the corner of his eye he could see the two men, so he took his drink with him and sat down at the table.

'Do you enjoy your job, Andy,' said the older man.

'It's a senior post in the civil service and is relatively well paid, so what's not to like? '

'It's just that you've been doing it a long time and I think I'd find it tedious doing the same job as long as you have done this, but I suppose we're all different. Now, having been able to give proper consideration to the suggestion we made the other evening about raising funds to support the business and home of your son Karl, are you willing to come on board?'

'I'm intrigued as to know how you discovered all this.'

'You and me alike, Andy. Paul here has a degree in computer studies. He tells me it's not at all difficult but when he tries to explain I'm utterly and completely lost. Most people, he says, even after all this time and all the warnings, fail to take their Internet security seriously even if they think they have. He's a useful member of the team is Paul – doesn't smoke, doesn't drink and, believe it or not, doesn't use drugs.'

'What sort of merchandise will I be dealing with?'

'The usual: Spice, cannabis and cocaine, the choice of our political masters.'

'You know I ought to be going to the police or the Ministry of Justice with all this?'

'Definitely. And if you decide to do that, you and they will see neither hide nor hair of us. But somehow I think we can do a deal otherwise you wouldn't have come back here tonight.'

'Okay, tell me how it works and when do we start?'.

'On Monday morning, Mrs Wilson will receive a parcel delivered by Paul and with it a briefcase that almost exactly matches your own into which the parcel will go. On Tuesday morning take it to work with you and when you get there, remove all your papers and anything else you do not wish to be seen. You go on your rounds at 9.30 leaving the briefcase on the chair by your door. That's all you have to do provided you remain away from your office for 10 minutes.. At the end of the day you go home as usual, stopping for a pint on the way. That will happen every week, and if your wife does not wish to handle the goods, she should show Paul where she wants it to be kept for your return. In the meantime, as a good will gesture you will find that five grand has gone into your No.2 ISA account.'

'How the hell . . .?'

'Don't ask, because I don't know either.'

'Apart from making money which I'm sure you do, not being a registered charity, why do you do this?'

'Yes, it's a business, of course it is. You will know better than me that drugs are an everyday part of life in most prisons where the numbers of inmates and staff mean security cannot be as it is in your place. Most of those inside were regular users before they arrived. Dealers provide a service and sometimes at great risk. Your place and one or two others I could name, have stringent security measures and yet your inmates are the most needy because they're stuck in there for years and need something to ease the pain of it. You will laugh cynically when I say I am providing a service, but I am, and I learned this from my son when he was doing his six months.'

'Do you not think that given what some of them have done means they deserve what they get without the anaesthetic of smuggled drugs?'

'That's a fair point and I would happily see them hang, but I just work the system as it is.'

Linda was completely charmed by Paul. He was intelligent and what the young call 'fit', just chatting about the things they both liked over a cup of coffee she made for him. He made her laugh, even when talking over with her the part she might play in the process. Although she was considerably older than him she had at once been attracted by him, and when he left, found herself looking forward to his next visit. It was on that second visit that Paul asked: 'Would you like to show me your bedroom?' a fantasy she had been nursing since his first visit. "That Monday morning feeling" would soon take on a very different meaning for her.

Even as he was parking his car on the first Tuesday, Andy considered going straight to his office and calling the police. All he would need to say was that he had been leading his paymasters on, with the intention of then handing it all over to the police and the justice department. Even as he went through the gate, and greeted the staff, this was what he was intending to do. But then he remembered that not only had he already received £5000 and passed it on to Karl, which changed things considerably and by the time he arrived at his office and greeted his secretaries, he knew it was too late. Quite who their inside man was, he had no idea. Presumably that person entered his office in his absence, removed the goods from the briefcase and distributed them to those who had arranged for their families to make payments to the providers. Not knowing which member of his staff this was created difficulties. It meant someone on the inside knew what he was doing.

After the early meeting of senior staff and reading through the reports of the night staff, they went their way other than Myles who usually stayed behind a short while to discuss any confidential matters that might have arisen. The two of them then set off on the morning rounds. There were more chances for prisoners to be out of their cells at this time of day, many of them functioning in the workshops in a variety of ways. By the time Andy returned to his office, almost an hour had passed and on examining the briefcase he discovered that whatever had been in there was now gone.

It was the prison chaplain, Angus Smallwood, who first detected the smell which he knew only too well from his days in Leeds prison, but which, on the whole, was not something he had ever smelt here, and he assumed that the smell was that of marijuana. Being of a liberal disposition, Angus was not immediately minded to do anything about it. He had himself smoked the stuff at university and he knew a good number of people, now occupying important positions in society used cocaine on a regular basis. Its use, he knew, was widespread, so the presence of weed certainly wasn't a hanging offence. He did feel, on reflection, that he ought to say something to someone, and the someone he chose was the deputy governor, Myles Hammond.

'Hello Angus, how's the wonderful world of religion treating you?'

'Well, apart from in here, I have no contact with it at all.'

'If you don't mind me saying so, I can hardly blame you. We may be struggling in the prison service in so many ways but at least our numbers are growing and from what I read your numbers are not. And I have to say, and I am not including you in this, it doesn't surprise me. In so many ways the church is stuck in the past, mostly in the age of the Reformation, and although attempts have been made to dress it up and apply all sorts of ridiculous make up, what people still profess to believe is little more than sixteenth century fantasy. No doubt it works for some, just as imaginary friends work for children, but surely we have to grow up.'

'You obviously feel that quite strongly and perhaps object to my presence and that of all chaplains in prisons, even though to a greater degree than you can know, I agree with you. And although it would be fascinating to continue this conversation, and at some time I would like to do so, not because I want to defend the institution but because such conversations are important, that's not why I've dropped in to see you.'

'That's a pity because thus far it's been the highlight of my day. So what can I do for you?'

'When I was in Leeds, and it is the same in many other places,

The Culture Of Deceit

we had a major issue with drugs. There is nothing new about that I know. When I came here, the first thing I realised was that it was not a problem of the same proportions and with all staff and visitors being subjected to the search and sniff regime, I can understand why. However, for the last couple of days something olfactory has made its presence felt.

'Oh?'

'I noticed it in A wing first. It was something more than tobacco, something I remembered only too well from Leeds and which is probably marijuana. You could argue that if it is, there is not much harm in it and you and I both probably partook at university without too much damage, but it does mean that it is getting in despite stringent security.'

'It has to be visitors or staff,' said Myles. 'If I was looking for suspects its most likely to be me or the boss as neither of us are searched or sniffed on our way in, but I can assure you it's not me and there's no chance it's the boss, so if you're right and it is getting in we shall have to consider possible ways that it might be happening, but that's going to be a big job and one that won't be at all popular with the staff. Everything would have to be examined including the food that is brought in – to see if it's concealed in the carrots for example.

'I think the best way forward is for me to have a word with Andy and see what he thinks we ought to do, but before then I would like to do some olfactory research myself. I'm not doubting you Angus, but like you I think I can recognise the smells from my time in Norwich and Strangeways. The boss may want to have a word with you, but at this stage I don't think there's any need for you to do anything else other than to keep your nostrils open as I shall do.'

'Thanks Myles. I'd like to hope I was wrong but no doubt in the course of things I'll hear something.'

He left the office and went down the stairs to find two inmates awaiting his return outside his own office. They had expressed an interest in being baptised, which if he knew anything about these two, would almost certainly be some part of a scam, knowledge of which he would have none. He invited them in.

Chapter Nine

It was the turn of Emily to go to London, staying overnight with Nicky and Claire, primarily so she could meet with Ivor and Nicky at The Poetry House to discuss and decide about the cover and layout of her forthcoming new volume. Everything she had ever had published had gone through the hands of these two highly experienced publishers. Ivor worked in the building's basement and Oliver, who once ran the institution, sometimes spoke of him as a troglodyte but he also knew that he was at the very top of his profession and that when the letters PH appeared on the spine of a book, everyone who knew about these things, knew that Ivor had been at work and that it would all be very good.

As Alex had found on his own recent visit to London, Emily realised that much though she adored her husband and children, to have this time completely away from them was a wonder to be thoroughly enjoyed. Their weaning was now complete, making it possible for her to get away. The only thing she hoped was that she would not arrive back at Sheffield station in the same state as Alex had been on his return from Banklyn. On the previous day he had received an outpatients appointment at the Hallamshire to see "a member of the team" in the psychiatric department. Alex had said he very much hoped it would be one of the cleaners whom he thought a very important member of the team. Amy told him he should cancel the appointment and Emily more or less thought the same though had not as yet said so.

She knew well enough that Alex was a very clever but complex person and from a perfunctory glimpse at the book titles he was reading knew that he was still on a spiritual journey of some sort or other. This was something of a closed world to her. She had never had a religious feeling or longing in her life. It had been all around her at Oxford, each college with its own chapel and chaplain, but never once had she felt any desire to explore a single aspect of it, and it remained the one part of their life they couldn't share, even talk about it because it was so difficult to find a language in common, though to be fair, in practice there was nothing in particular to be shared. Alex had made it abundantly clear that he no longer had any interest in Christianity or the Church no matter what else he might wish to develop for himself. She did sometimes think, however, that the Mother Superior, as she sometimes laughingly called her mother, was trying surreptitiously to get Alex back into the church. She smiled at the thought but all the same Amy had to be watched!

Leaving St Pancras she took a cab to the flat shared by Nicky and Claire. As yet Nicky was not home, but Claire greeted her warmly.

'Please forgive me, Claire, if you have already told me and I have forgotten, but do you work and if so, what work do you do?'

'I'm what's called a professional proofreader and I work for publishers specialising in books concerning mathematics, in which, they are relieved to know, I am equipped with two degrees. It's a very demanding job in terms of concentration as you can probably imagine and I have to spend most of my time working my way through equations of one kind or another. It's very specialist work and mistakes have to be spotted.'

'Is it the editors who are responsible for the errors?'

'Nearly always, but sometimes the writer gets something wrong. That's what I really like. I call them up and innocently ask if what they have written is what they intended to write. It's a different process altogether to proofreading a novel or even poetry, and so I charge a great deal.'

'All that concentration must be exhausting at the end of the day.'

'It would be if I foolishly tried to work right through, so I make sure I have breaks, sometimes long breaks and go out into town, perhaps to have lunch with Nicky or do some shopping. Unless Nicky is out, I never work in the evening and at the weekend I only do so on Saturday mornings.'

'What form do the proofs come to you in?'

'Always online now, though because I'm working with so many symbols and numbers I can only do it making use of special programs, though as I made extensive use of them during my MSc it's been relatively straightforward. And you can see the size of the monitor I need and use.

'Where did you go?'

'Cambridge and UCL.'

'What sort of other openings are there?'

'Loads. The country is crying out for specialist mathematicians and if I get up tomorrow, I know full well that there would be work just around the corner, but not work I could do at home and not work as well paid.'

'You sound happy Claire.'

'You know about the joy that comes from being in love. That undergirds everything I am about, so what's not to be happy about?'

At that moment Emily's phone rang. It was Amy.

'Everything's fine but I'm sending you a photo of your sofa.'

'The sofa?'

'Well really it's a photo of what's on it. I think you'll be amused. How was the journey?'

'Straightforward and I'm with Claire now and I imagine Nicky will be here soon.'

'Good, well enjoy the taste of freedom.'

'I am!'

Moments later an email arrived with an attachment which showed a sofa, and on it in the middle, the former Bishop of Truro fast asleep with his two children also asleep, one on each side and tucked into him.

'Claire, do come and see this.'

'That is wonderful. You must get it printed and framed. If you like I'll print it for you now, just send it to me by Airdrop.'

In no time at all, especially with a colour laser printer, a photo taken in Derbyshire moments ago had already been printed in London. "Whatever will they think of next?" thought Emily to herself with a grin.

'We thought we'd go out to eat,' said Claire, 'but not to a girls' club, if you take my meaning. You'd be far too much of an attraction.'

'I could always carry the photo of my husband and children with me.'

'So could quite a few others, believe me.'

'I love Nicky, even if not in the way you do. She has an astonishing mind and a capacity to see and understand what I'm writing. I dare say that all publishers have to have that, but there's a particular quality to her work I admire greatly. How did you meet, if you don't mind me asking?'

'Of course not. It was a pure fluke so obviously meant to be. We had adjacent seats at Covent Garden when the Bolshoi came to do a short season. At the first interval she turned and asked if I fancied a drink? We went outside and went to the *Marquess of Anglesey* and didn't return. We were fascinated by each other and immediately attracted.'

'Was the Ballet any good?'

'Superb, at least what we saw of it, but the ticket was not wasted, was it?'

The lock on the door was turned and in came Nicky. She and Emily hugged one another.

'So how's my favourite poet?'

'I bet you say that to all the girls.'

'No. Only to you because you are the best, and if they hadn't needed to appoint a male heterosexual after Carol Ann Duffy, you would have been the best of all poets laureate.'

'I think that what you mean is that it would have increased your sales!'

'I've met Simon Armitage a few times and I'm really pleased for him because he's a really nice man, but a beautiful young mum would have been even better.'

She turned to Claire and held and kissed her.

'How's my lovely mathematical genius?'

'Thinking of giving it up and becoming a poet.'

'You'll never get a publisher.'

'Oh, I don't know. There was one in bed with me only this morning drinking tea.'

They all laughed.

On their way back after their meal, and just about 200 meters from home, two young men stopped them in the street and it was clear they had been drinking.

'Well, well, well,' said one of them. 'Three lezzies out together and now going back for a threesome. We'll come and watch and then show you how it should be done, but give us a foretaste here and now. Go on, you dirty slags, start touching each other.'

'I don't think you can say 'dirty slags' as it's pretty close to being an oxymoron,' said Nicky, now in the role of a teacher. 'Who was your English teacher? I probably know her.'

'You mean you're teachers?'

'Yes, and Mrs Elliot at the end there has two small twin children to get back to.'

'Twins?' said the other. 'I'm a twin and my brother works on the tube. How old are your twins?'

'I'll show you a photo of them and my husband fast asleep,' said Emily and drew out her phone. Both young men looked.

'What are they called?'

'Chloe and George, and that's the order in which they came out.'

'What do you teach?' said one to Claire.

'Maths and Higher Maths.'

'Shit, you must be clever. I was useless at maths.'

'Actually, you're not useless at maths as no one is, it's just that you weren't taught properly. I'm serious and it makes me so cross that men like you grow up thinking you're useless at something when it could have been totally different.'

'So is this a teacher's night out then?'

'It is exactly that,' said Nicky. 'A chance to let our hair down and escape from children and husbands.'

They all laughed.

'Well, thanks for talking with us and I apologise for what we said at the start.'

'We hear worse in the classroom, believe you me,' said Nicky as they began to walk the last few metres to their house, saving their laughter until the front door was closed.

'We can laugh,' said Claire, 'but it might not have turned out quite so well. Male sexuality must be pretty grim, driven as they are by inner forces which just seem to possess them. What's worse is that some women seem to want to be like that too as if it were something to aspire to.'

'It used to be said, though how true it is I don't know, that in the army bromide was put into their tea to suppress sexual urges.

Perhaps we could start a protest movement demanding that bromide be put in the water, except in Derbyshire,' said Emily.

Angus Smallwood sat watching his television but not seeing anything. Nothing had come of his conversation with the deputy governor now some weeks ago, so today he went upstairs and knocked on the door of the governor himself who had, at least, given the impression he was pleased to see him. He repeated all that he had said to Myles. In response the governor had nodded and smiled and said that Myles had spoken about this to him and that together they had visited the areas where Angus thought he had smelt the presence of drugs but discovered nothing at all. He had said to Angus that of course prisons were smelly places even on a good day and that long-term male prisoners notoriously did not take care with regard to personal hygiene. He had been giving a lot of thought as to how drugs could get in given the precautions they had in place with such good sniffer dogs. He also said that he would take it as a personal insult if their precautions were somehow being bypassed given the thought and attention that had gone into putting them into place. He was however hugely grateful to Angus for being attentive to the possibility that drugs might have been smuggled into the place and had decided that a major review of practice should be carried out.

It was clear to Angus that he was being completely fobbed-off and in effect told that how the prison ran itself was not his affair. Despite the smiles from the governor he was under no illusion as to what Andy thought about religion in prisons, that he regarded it as nothing more than a hobby but one that he would like to have stopped because dangerous. This referred to followers of all religious traditions which he thought warped the minds of the vulnerable and he had openly told Angus on a number of occasions that he did not think it was the responsibility of the prison service to recruit for the Church of England.

What most concerned Angus however was not the negative views of the governor on the church, for his own went far beyond them, it was what he felt was a cover-up and a deliberate refusal to face facts. He knew without a doubt that it was not smelly armpits and socks that he had detected, but marijuana and possibly also spice, though he was less certain of the latter. Perhaps Andy and Myles had decided between them not to make a fuss, so that when the Inspector of Prisons came, they could report that all was well and as far as they knew, drug-free, even if they admitted the possibility that sometimes a tiny amount of marijuana got in, usually via visitors and passed from mouth to mouth during a kiss.

Angus was not given to conspiracy theories, and knew it was quite possible that he was mistaken, though he doubted that, but once the governor and deputy governor had decided to take it no further, he himself had no leverage, no power or authority to question their decision, and he knew that his functioning in the place depended wholly on their goodwill, which on the whole they had to give him no matter what they felt personally because of the way the prison service worked. They could not merely request his move, but if they chose, demand it and almost certainly Andy Wilson knew that. So, perhaps this was the moment the book of Ecclesiastes spoke of when it said there was a time to keep silence. In any case the presence or otherwise of drugs in the prison was not even slightly a part of his remit as the chaplain. There was a Chaplain General, Archdeacon somebody or other, whom he supposed he could telephone and discuss it with, but the chances were that in the present climate when fewer governors wanted such a figure under their feet, he would tell him to concentrate on doing his own job and leave other matters to the governor.

When he had begun working with them, Andy received a number he should call if a meeting was required for any reason. When he did so, he was told he would be contacted and met in the usual place. He had been told that he must always stick to his normal routine and so had continued going into the Bluebell on his way home for a pint. There were a few locals but there was no sign of the man or men he had previously met, so he drank his beer and read a newspaper that had been left on the table in front of him.

'I wouldn't read that rubbish if I was you, Andy,' said a voice he recognised, and when he put down the paper he could see a familiar face.

'You asked for a meeting.'

'We have a padre, a chaplain, who is proving to be a real pain in the arse. He used to work in a local prison and, he says, there he became used to the smell of marijuana and spice. He says he can now smell it in certain areas of the prison, and I have assured him that neither my deputy nor myself have been able to smell anything other than the disgusting bodies of some of our inmates whose ideas of cleanliness would not be yours or mine. I've also made it clear that he is involving himself in a matter outside his own job description, and that he should leave the matter to Myles and me. Now he's not a prison appointee so I can't just sack him, though I would like to do so and not have him replaced but I did just wonder what you thought about this as the last thing that I want to happen is that it screws up our business arrangement.'

'You're right but there's no need to worry. Leave it with me.'

Chapter Ten

It had been a good day. Her meeting with Ivor and Nicky made her realise that writing was worth all the effort and agonising when she saw her words looking so well presented on the page, and then to see a number of possible covers which Ivor had produced following chats with her on the phone of which she had with great difficulty eventually chosen one.

There had also been a great surprise for her when Nicky said that the *Poetry House* was undertaking a new venture whereby the best living poets would be asked to produce an edition of one of the great poets of a previous age together with a substantial critical introduction to their works.

'I would like you to do the first. It should of course be undertaken by me, but I concede to your skills as a poet, and so I hope you might be willing to do the man we both adore.'

'John Donne might not be your ideal bedtime partner, Nicky, and even I might hesitate if we had to share the bed with a flea, but it's you and only you who are equipped to write this book. I can't do it because I would know throughout that there was someone who could do it so very much better.'

'But I'm not a poet.'

'Who in this country knows more about poetry than you. I'm obviously somewhat gutted to be saying this, but Nicky, this is yours.'

'Oh Emily, you are wonderful and ever so generous, but it can't be. For me to publish a work of my own in my own publishing house would be looked on somewhat askance by my rivals and responded to critically. No it has to be you, not least because you're the only one I could trust to do it. Your former fans – those you encountered at Hay – will no doubt see it as a further sign that you have sold out to the establishment, but you and I know that it isn't so. So please say Yes.'

'Reluctantly I do so, provided that when you see what I am producing you don't immediately tear it into shreds.'

'But that's the point. With you doing it I shall know in advance that it is going to be very good indeed, though obviously not quite as good as I would do it.'

'Modestly put.'

They gave each other a hug and just for one tiny moment Emily could feel the sort of tingle that women might feel for one another.

Later, on the train home Emily found herself almost bursting with excitement. The prospect of time with John Donne thrilled her heart. She had wanted to do something like this ever since she first read him and he worked his magic on her. She also wondered about the magic Nicky had worked on her today, that moment, and it was no more than that, when she felt goosebumps as they hugged one another and was truly surprised because she had only ever felt anything like that with Alex. Perhaps it was nothing more than her mounting joy at the prospect of the former Dean of St Paul's and she knew how totally committed she was to and constantly attracted by her husband, so perhaps it was nothing to be concerned about, besides which in a very short time her life would once again be taken over by Chloe and George. London had been wonderful and the freedom she had enjoyed meant a great deal to her, but home was where she belonged, even though she would have to warn everyone that a new man was moving in with her, though Alex would say that the man had been living with them already for a long time, and Emily knew it was so, and as she thought about it she recognised that the frisson of excitement she had felt with Nicky was really all about Donne. Or was it?

Most of the way home in the car was taken up with Emily talking nineteen to the dozen about her new project, and about her new book with its wonderful cover and layout, and about her time with Claire and Nicky, including their encounter with the two youths.

'Were you not anxious when that happened?' asked Alex.

'I was, as they really were quite horrible, but then Nicky took charge, became their schoolteacher, then Claire became their maths teacher and encouraged them to believe they were certainly more capable than any teacher at school had made them feel, and suddenly they were transformed into nice young men.'

'I'm pleased to hear it. Well by the time we get home, two little creatures who are very excited that mummy is coming home, will have been fed and had their bath and be waiting for you. It's difficult to know whether they or I have missed you most but as I have no toys to distract me, I'm pretty sure it's me. All the same, I'm glad it's gone as well as it has, and between you and me, I genuinely think you will be better on John Donne than Nicky.'

'Oh darling, it's wonderful to be back even after just one day away, to be with you again, though a strange thing happened early this afternoon after Nicky had told me about the book. We gave one another a hug before I left, and for a brief instant and it was no more than that, I felt a tingle as we held one another.'

'Why not? You're extremely close and share a great deal. You trust one another implicitly so why is it not possible to feel love for someone? It would seem to me pretty normal. After all you have regularly to put up with the obvious fact that I very much love your mother, but it doesn't trouble me because not for one moment can she replace you. But it's so wonderful that you told me this and I'm delighted.'

'Thank you my love. No wonder the Archbishop of Canterbury hates you!'

Once the children were in bed, and Amy had returned home in Sheffield, husband and wife sat together on the sofa, Emily excitedly telling Alex how she thought she might tackle the book on John Donne.

'His love poems are of course in a class of their own and no one has ever matched them and now that you're a married woman I feel confident you will do more than justice to them and already I'm looking forward to what you have to say. But a large part of his output, in poetry and prose, is his spiritual writing, his religious poems, many of which I think brilliant, but how are you going to tackle those? You can't exactly ignore them or regard them as secondary.'

'You're quite right. To be honest I haven't really begun to think how to deal with them. I've tended to concentrate on the love poems and his work on suicide: *Biathanatos*. So I guess I am going to have to do some serious reading of his other works.'

'I hope you know I will help you wherever I can, but there's only one poet in this house and it's not me.'

'It's always been something of an irony that the greatest critics have largely been quite unable to write themselves. Some feel that they can thereby dismiss anything they say, but I disagree, so I think your expertise may well prove not just helpful but essential.'

The cries of a baby discontinued their conversation as Emily went upstairs to respond and Alex turned on the television for the late evening news headlines. He then turned it off, together with the lights and followed Emily upstairs. George was asleep again and Emily preparing for bed. As she undressed, he stood behind her and put his arms around her. She turned to him.

'I reckon you've got about half an hour to prove I'm not on the turn,' she said with a giggle.

'Half an hour?' he replied. 'When I see you like this, I'll be lucky to last a few minutes!'

For Linda, Monday mornings lasted much longer than half-an-hour when she began to realise just how much she had been missing out on in earlier years. God only knows, she thought, where Paul acquired such incredible skills, but Andy had certainly never had any of them. The other good news came when Joan, her daughter-in-law rang to say that thanks to them both the house and the business had been secured and that they didn't know how to say thank you enough. When Linda replied that it was her pleasure, little did Joan know what she was talking about.

In the prison, Andy was totally at ease with his Tuesday morning routine. The chaplain never bothered him now with anxieties about drugs and he seemed to be convinced when Andy told him that a full review had now been held and nothing untoward discovered. The end result as far as Andy was concerned was that Angus had been put in his place and shut up. Angus, for his part, remained unconvinced. In part this arose when he saw something being passed during the service in the prison chapel. He knew what was going on, and those involved knew he knew what was going on, but felt he was unlikely to do anything about it, because his credibility depended on every priest's biggest need: to be liked. Here he was on to a winner because he was popular among inmates.

By now Angus was well aware that he could not take his concerns to either the governor or the deputy governor which, of course, was the only place he was allowed to take them. He was bound by the Official Secrets Act and could do nothing about that. But worst of all was having to come to terms with the possibility that the person bringing drugs into the establishment might be its head or his deputy, the only ones neither search nor sniffed. Perhaps to prove a point, both men now voluntarily submitted to this every Monday, Wednesday and Friday and were always clean. On Tuesdays and Thursdays they needed to get on with their rounds without hold-ups, as everyone understood. After a couple of weeks of this regime they were approached by one of the senior officers who told them that they should revert to the previous practice of not being searched or sniffed, as increasingly those responsible felt somewhat embarrassed that the governor and deputy governor should be treated in this way. And so they stopped.

Alex was preparing to take a second trip out to Banklyn. With the children now getting used to being each day with Fiona, Amy offered to travel with Alex, spending the day in Beverley, a place she had always wanted to visit.

'What you really mean is that you are anxious lest I collapse on the way back like last time and think that I need someone to pick up the pieces.'

'Yes,' said Amy, 'that's more or less it.'

'I was joking, Amy.'

'And I'm not prepared to take the risk. If you say that I can't come, then I shall nevertheless sit in the same railway carriage and probably in the next seat to you, and I shall await your return to the station, and repeat my practice on the way back.'

'Do you know, you are even worse than your daughter and that is saying something in terms of being utterly bossy. I think I shall adopt Emily's practice of calling you Mother Superior, and if you do indeed come with me on the train, I will use the words so everyone can hear.'

'I'll take that as a Yes then. When do we leave?'
'In about 10 minutes time.'

On the slow train Amy told Alex a little more about her former life as a teacher, after she had left the convent which he had known little about and then had an interesting discussion about the merits or otherwise of *Ulysses*, the modernist novel by James Joyce. In the end they agreed they didn't like it nor anything by the modernists including *The Wasteland* though they recognised that it was a clever book.

'So what's today's agenda?'

'Only to see the person allocated to me,' said Alex, aware that they were in a public place.

'Will your recent trip to the Lake District be mentioned?'

'I have to play that by ear as I haven't actually received any guidance.'

'And you'll get a taxi back to Beverley station and let me know at what time you will be arriving.'

'Yes and thank you so very much for coming with me today. If by any chance what happened last time happens again then I shall know that I have to give this work up.'

'And have you done anything yet about your appointment at the Hallamshire?'

'No, and the appointment is next week.'

'You think you might attend?'

'I know you think I probably shouldn't, and that I have other matters to which I ought to attend as a priority, but I'm aware that on two occasions now I've been given senior positions, and twice pulled out of them. It might just help to have someone help me to understand why these things have happened, and if that doesn't prove to be the case, then I can quite easily prevent any further appointments.'

'Oh Alex, be careful.'

After stopping everywhere in the East Riding and one or two other places as well, their train finally pulled into Beverley station. Alex took a cab and Amy used her feet to take her shopping in the town centre and to visit the lovely Minster. Once Alex was through security, he collected his keys and made for the governor's office but was stopped en route by Angus Smallwood.

'Is there any chance we could have a private conversation before you leave?' asked Angus.

'That shouldn't be a problem. Once I've seen Armstrong I'll let the governor know you and I are going to have a chat.'

'That may not be wise for reasons I'll make clear later. You could say I've offered you my office in which to write up your notes before you leave. Anyway it's important that we meet and as surreptitiously as possible.'

Alex was puzzled but put it out of his mind as he approached Andy's room, where a prison officer was emerging who greeted Alex and went on his way. Andy was not there but as his open brief case was, he assumed he must be somewhere about the place. A secretary came in.

'Ah, Dr Elliot,' she said, 'how good to see you again. The governor and assistant governor are doing their rounds, but he says he hopes you will stay long enough to see him after you've finished.'

'Thank you. I shall get on with it then.'

'You have to be accompanied going to the cell of a prisoner, so I'll find someone to do that.'

She left and Alex sat down to wait. He had brought with him a book to read, *The Rules and Exercises of Holy Dying* usually shortened to just the final two words. It was published in 1651 and the work of Jeremy Taylor, at the time someone keeping a very low profile with Oliver Cromwell still in charge, but who, following the Restoration of 1660, became a Bishop in Ireland.

Reading it, thought Alex, would not suit everyone (to say the least) but as a work of devotion it had not been surpassed.

It took ten minutes for an officer to emerge and lead Alex towards Armstrong's cell. As before the door was left partially open with the bolt preventing closure.

There was no pretence at any kind of greeting. Once Alex had sat down, Armstrong said, 'Have you had any word yet about my release date?'

'At the present time the only person talking about your release is you. The rest of us have to prepare for the Parole Board and, as you know, they could quite easily decide not to give you parole.'

'Do you know what your report will say?'

'There are two answers to that. The first is that I have yet to complete all my allotted tasks and so cannot yet make a report, the second is that you will not have access to it.'

'My legal representative came to see me last week. She's already thinking that she is going to appeal to the Court of human rights if I'm not given parole because all statements and documents should be available to me as of right.'

'Well, I know nothing about how the law works and as I'm not actually going to be a member of the Board, and so not casting a vote, it won't be my concern.'

'As I said last time you came, I've done 20 years here and in Wakefield, and to be perfectly honest I deserved it, but now is the beginning of the rest of my life and the only place I can live it is on the outside, not in here.'

'After abducting Anna and Rose, you raped and murdered them both. What did you do then?'

'That's a very odd question, if you don't mind me saying so. I'm in here not because of what I did afterwards but because of what I did in the first place.'

'Okay then, humour me. What did you do then?'

'As far as I can recall, and we're talking about something that happened 21 years ago, I went downstairs and made myself a drink so that I could sit and think about what I'd done and what was to be done now.'

'And that presumably was how the police found you when they broke in your door.'

'Yes. I knew that I had done something bad, and I had no idea what I should do further.'

'Something "bad" was it? Perhaps two little girls might have thought it better described as total evil.'

Armstrong shrugged.

'Why did you not open the door when the police were doing their door-to-door search?'

'As I understand it, your presence here is to make an assessment here and now, and not to question me about things I already admitted in court.'

'Gosh, I wonder who told you that. My brief from the Parole Board is to ask any questions I want that will enable me to make a report to those considering your application. I can ask whatever I like. If you choose not to answer any particular questions, I will make note of that and include them in the report. So, it's up to you, and I ask again why you did not answer the door when the police knocked?'

'I've no idea. I was a long time ago.'

'What was your relationship to the parents of Rose and Anna whom you raped and murdered?'

Armstrong stared malevolently at Alex.

'You've been to see them, haven't you?'

'I will ask again: what was your relationship to Tom and Mattie Kiernan, the parents of Rose and Anna whom you raped and murdered?'

'I didn't have one. I knew my neighbours, and I even filled a casual vacancy on the Parish Council but I never found people all that friendly towards me.'

'Why do you think that might have been?'

'You'd have to ask them.'

'Is it true that you liked to hang around the bus stop when the girls got off on their way home from school?'

'I'm sure you've read the transcript of the trial when this was put to me but I'll repeat myself. No, I did nothing of the sort, except when I was intending to catch the bus myself, but no doubt someone saw me and decided I was up to no good and was some kind of pervert.'

'Though of course they were absolutely right to think that, weren't they, or do you not regard the rape of a six-year-old and an eight-year-old as the work of a pervert?'

Armstrong did not reply.

'The pathologist reported that you slit the throats of the two girls. That suggests you must have had a knife with you, and therefore premeditated.'

'Oh you've become a lawyer now, have you? Just about the only job you haven't had yet.'

'Was it premeditated, Armstrong?'

'What gives you the right to come in here and ask questions like these?'

He was sounding aggressive.

'Was it premeditated?'

'Just piss off and get out of here. I won't answer any more of your fucking questions.'

'I should remind you that you are the one who has applied for parole and I can for certain tell you that failure to answer questions will not help your application.'

The cell door opened and in came a prisoner officer.

'Is everything ok, Dr Elliot? I happened to be passing and heard Armstrong's angry outburst. On behalf of the prison I apologise.'

'I'm fine thanks and Armstrong has helped me more than he

might imagine this morning. It will make writing my report that much easier. He's by no means the figure he likes to present us all with.'

Alex stood and left the cell and made his way towards the governor's office. Behind him he heard the officer say to Armstrong, "You're a nasty bag of shit, Armstrong. It's a great pity you can't be hanged. You should be".

Andy was on the phone but waved Alex in, and magically coffee appeared from somewhere brought by Andy's secretary.

'How was that?' asked Andy one he had finished the phone call.

'Well, we had a breakthrough. He lost his cool and wasn't the quiet and completely controlled person I saw last time. I feel it truly is a front, just as I think he put on during his trial, and as you and your staff have thought him to be doing.'

'Have you met the parents of the girls yet?'

'Yes and needless to say they have been destroyed by him just as much as he destroyed their two girls.'

'There's no date set for the Board yet, but it must be happening soon. Will you need to come again?'

'Not to see Armstrong, but I shall need to speak to a few of your staff who have had dealings with him. I think I know what you think about him, and that one of your men who came in when he heard Armstrong swearing at me, has also made it clear how he feels about him, and I don't blame him, Andy. Your chaplain has offered me the use of his office to allow me to write up my notes before I leave so I'll take my leave. It would be a kindness if you could select five of your staff to meet with me next time. But I must say again, how much I admire you and all your staff working here. You must all have to exercise considerable restraint much of the time.'

'That's true Dr Elliot and thank you for your expression of support. But before you go there's one matter on which I would welcome your thoughts, in total confidence of course, concerning Revd Smallwood. I think he may have lost his way as a chaplain and is just time-serving, but see what you think.'

'That's quite outside my brief.'

'I know and nothing will be recorded, but you've had contact with vicars in the past and it would help me a great deal if you could offer your thoughts on what I should do, if anything.'

'He's not your appointment as I understand it.'

'That's right, but I can request a different chaplain and ask that the present man be transferred.'

Alex smiled enigmatically and left.

Chapter Eleven

Alex sat down next to Angus.

'How did it go with Armstrong today?'

'He's not the nicest of men, though possibly one of the more deceitful. But you asked me to pop in for a word and here I am, though you must understand that I am functioning outside my brief and that I could be asked to leave at any moment by the governor.'

'Yes, of course I do and I'm hugely grateful that you're willing to give me a hearing even if, given your position here, you will not be able to do anything about what I tell you, but I feel I have to tell someone and so far both Andy and Myles have chosen to ignore me.

'These ultramodern high security prisons have instituted all the paraphernalia to prevent the smuggling in of mobile phones and drugs, which are the curse of most other prisons. In my time here this has not been much of a problem. From time to time something gets in, usually weed, but in pretty small quantities and nothing is normally done about it as it's on a very small-scale. But something has changed. The first thing that struck me when I came here from Leeds was the absence of familiar smells. As you know in some prisons many of the officers are being affected by the presence of certain drugs, mainly spice, but that isn't the case here, or at least it wasn't, and as I say, something has changed.

'I began to be aware of this some time ago and reported the matter upstairs, and both Andy and Myles went to sniff the air and reported that they could detect nothing, and when I've mentioned this on subsequent occasions, their response has been the same. Now I would fully understand this if the matter in hand was an inspection and wish to report that no drugs are getting in or being used. That would give them both a Sunday school sticker in their book. But I happen to think that somehow or other quite a lot of drugs are now getting in here.'

'When I come,' said Alex, 'I'm subjected to a search and the attention of one of two spaniels, and I thought that everyone was, staff and visitors alike.'

'You're almost correct, but not quite. Neither the governor nor his deputy are subject to that. No one else, whether you are from the Parole Board, anyone from the Prison Inspectorate or any staff member in whatever capacity, is given exemption. I think, eliminating all other possibilities, what is happening is being organised by either of those who do not receive the attention that others do. But, because it's not possible for one or other of these men to go around distributing in the manner of Father Christmas, it's clear to me that there must be somebody else working on the inside who does that for them, presumably a prison officer.'

'Angus, where should you be taking this concern?'

'To the governor or his deputy.'

'From your experience can tell me how it works financially? I know prisoners earn money in their workshops and so on but surely not enough to be buying drugs and making it worth the while of someone taking the risk of getting them in. So what happens?'

'Those organising this on the outside are in regular contact with those who visit most often, and they convey to the prisoners the information about what might be available. Most prisoners will jump at this either for their own use or as a means of control in the prison, in much the same sort of way as snout was at one time. When the contract is agreed, it is signed and sealed by the visitor, and it is they who pay for the drugs, and usually through the nose to the suppliers who are usually less than friendly to those who do not pay up on time. From conversations I've had with old lags there's a lot of money in it.'

'I bet there is. But your chief suspects are very well paid and have got themselves into very good jobs. They would be risking an enormous amount and for what – money they don't actually need. It doesn't make sense.'

'But it doesn't always work like that, Alex. A lot of people in this world have vulnerabilities they largely conceal from prying eyes, even from the eyes of their spouses. These people are experts in doing their research by all accounts and can spot a vulnerability from a great distance, and on the whole that is what they work on. I really am not suggesting that either Andy or Myles is having an affair, has a serious gambling problem or regularly visits the red-light district of Hull, but you take my point. They will find a weakness if it is there.'

'I can't say anything in an official capacity, as you well know, and if I did so I rather think Andy would have me out, not just from Banklyn but from everything in the service and to be honest I could hardly blame him. But I do have a concern for your well-being and I require a little time to think things through and consider what might best be done. Believe it or not I'm not totally *persona non grata* among the great and the good and I can always ask questions that will reveal nothing whatsoever about circumstances here, but which may elicit the answers I'm seeking. But I am clear about one thing and that is to keep your head down and not mention drugs at all, and at all times to take good care of yourself. You may well be dealing with some rather

unpleasant people. I don't know what your vulnerabilities are, but *they* might well do.'
'I don't think finding out that I'm gay would take lot of investigation and attempt to blackmail me would be a waste of time.'
'All the same, take care!'

Having let Amy know he was now leaving the prison, Alex went over in his mind the conversation he had just had with Angus. The journey in the taxi was not long but he knew that he must give serious thought to all that Angus had said. He could see Amy waiting for him by the small taxi rank, and they had just a matter of 10 minutes to wait for their train.

'In his poem, *The Whitsun Weddings*,' said Alex to Amy, 'I imagine it was on this line that Philip Larkin encountered the newly married couples who make up the substance of his writing. Surely there should be a plaque at every stop. If I was a professor or a bishop, I would write a letter.'

'In which case, thank God you're not.'

'So have you had a good shopping expedition and were you able to get into the Minster?'

'Yes on both accounts. Good shops and a splendid mediaeval building without, thankfully, the crowds that would be filling York Minster today. I also bought some sandwiches and a pie for you as I had a feeling you were not meant to be eating there today.'

'Amy, what would I do without you? Thank you so much and as it happens, I'm very hungry.'

Once they were on the train and Alex had finished off his lunch washed down with a bottle of dandelion and burdock, which Alex said he had not drunk since he was a boy, she asked him how he was feeling after the day.'

'It's been much more revealing than I thought it might be but I don't think I need to come back to see the parole applicant, though I will have to come back once more to interview five members of staff. After that all I will have to do is complete my report and that will be it.'

'You're not required to be present when the decision is made?'

'No and I'm very glad about that.'

'Presumably they will let you know.'

'I imagine so, but as I haven't been through the process before, it's a matter of wait-and-see.'

'Well I have some news for you. Emily rang and asked me to tell you, because she knew you wouldn't be able to receive any calls, that the Hallamshire telephoned this morning with a cancellation, offering you the appointment – tomorrow morning. Your wife said yes.'

'Yes, well I knew it would happen eventually, that all my decisions would be made by my wife, but I had rather thought it wouldn't be until I was in my dotage though it occurs to me that she perhaps thinks I'm there now. As it happens, however, we've given a bit of thought to this and she knows that I had said I would go for one appointment and then see. What you've said to me, Amy, I'm not going to disregard, but I think I should at least turn up once before rejecting it. The spiritual task of which you have spoken will almost certainly take considerably longer than it will for me to drive into the Hallamshire tomorrow morning. By the way, did Emily tell you the time of my appointment.'

'10 o'clock.'

'That's good as it will give me time to take the children into their playgroup before I head off into Sheffield and I'll have to give thought in advance to where I might be able to park. I might be lucky at the hospital but I rather doubt it.'

'In which case you're in luck already. You're seeing someone called Dr Daly at the mental health centre on Prince of Wales Road. Apparently there's no problem with parking there and the sign outside simply says NHS Sheffield CCG. I've driven past it many times and it's just an ordinary building.'

'CCG stands for Clinical Commissioning Group. They asked me to serve on it in Truro but I left before I could do so. Well, I'll give it a whirl.'

'You're restless this evening, my darling. Are you alright?' asked Emily.

'I don't think it's a panic attack coming on, if that's what you're worried about, though it's very much concerned with my visit today, not about the prisoner but concerns a member of staff.'

'Does that mean you're able to talk about it or not?'

'Well I hardly think you're likely to report me for breaking the Official Secrets Act, and in any case I'm not altogether sure it's covered by it. Shortly before I left, I met with the chaplain because he asked for a meeting. It's quite outside the province of my presence there and I suppose we could have arranged to meet outside the prison but it was more convenient for both of us to speak there and then.

'Although he's been there sometime, he has worked in other prisons, those with a real drug problem and it's been said that prison officers have themselves been affected by the fumes coming from hallucinatory drugs that have been smuggled into the jail, and nobody seems to have the first idea how to stop it though it is also said that the prison officers are the ones who have smuggled drugs in there in the first place. At Banklyn, being a high security institution, the measures to prevent the smuggling in of mobile phones and drugs are considerable. When I go in and my appointment is from the Cabinet Office, I am searched and then a spaniel is let loose on me and the same happens to everyone going in, visitors and staff alike, but with two exceptions.

'On the basis of his previous experience in other prisons, the chaplain has begun to detect the smell which comes from drug use. Once he reported this to the governor, who with his deputy, went to the particular wing and used their noses but could detect nothing. Angus however, is convinced that either their noses are blocked or they are deliberately ignoring what is self-evident to him so that they can continue to earn brownie points with the Prisons Inspectorate.'

'It hardly seems much of a matter to get worked up about.'

'Yes, you're right and of course a high proportion of the population probably uses street drugs, including cigarettes and alcohol, and perhaps as a society we ought to be considering allowing such things into prisons which would of course help eliminate the criminal involvement of those who are supplying and breaking the law by smuggling, though to be honest I can't see any government seeking to do that any time soon. But in the present instance, the question of who is introducing illegal substances into Banklyn remains. That is what continues to concern Angus.

'He thinks that there can only be two people within the prison who are involved in this, two members of staff, one to import it and another to distribute it. He believes that the one bringing the stuff in must be one or other of the two exceptions I mentioned earlier. The distributor is most likely to be a prison officer. The two exceptions are the governor and deputy governor. They are not searched and sniffed.

'Just before I went to have my conversation this morning with Angus, following my interview with Armstrong, the governor hinted to me that he wanted rid of Angus. The way the prison services run means that the governor can't actually sack the chaplain but what he can do is ask for his transfer.'

'It could just be a coincidence,' said Emily, alarmed that Alex might be getting in over his head.

'Yes, it could, and in any case I don't think there's anything I can do about it. What goes on inside these places other than when someone applies for parole, is not the responsibility of the Parole Board, and it would be utterly foolish to poke my nose into what has nothing to do with me, though I suppose it's quite possible that I am only getting caught up in it because at the centre is a priest, and one who has not the first idea where to turn for help. If he was to go and see his bishop, he would most likely be told by him to go and organise an evangelical mission for prisoners and staff alike which would resolve all problems at a stroke.'

'Are you serious?'

'I'm afraid so. That's the sort of nonsense which drove me out of the church.'

'It's a good job it did though, otherwise we would never have met.'

'You're quite right my love and I don't regret it for one single moment, and each night when we lie in bed together I mouth a tiny "thank you" to our dear friend Oliver, to whom we owe a great deal.'

By 9:30 in the morning, the traffic in Sheffield had begun to settle down, as Alex made his way to the Prince of Wales Road and the NHS building where he was due to meet Dr Daly. Whether the doctor was a man or a woman he had no idea but presumed he would soon find out. He parked in the NHS car park and walked back around the front of the building and in through the main door. Reception consisted of a hole in the wall with protective perspex preventing physical contact.

'My name is Elliot and I have an appointment with Dr Daly at 10 o'clock.'

The young man on the other side looked at his computer screen.

'Dr Elliot I think. If you go through the door on the far side of this room, you will find a small waiting room on the right-hand side. Dr Daly will come and find you there, Dr Elliot.'

Alex did as he was told and was glad to leave what was quite a noisy waiting room and entered one in which he sat there alone. Before he had left home, and indeed before he had breakfast, Amy had called to wish him well and to remind him not to commit himself to anything he didn't actually choose.

A man appeared at the doorway. He was balding, portly and sported a rather magnificent long beard.

'Dr Elliot? Let's go and get a drink. By the way just in case you wondered, I'm Tony Daly, and I'm delighted to meet you and to be with you here this morning.'

The doctor turned right and Alex followed to a room at the end where they collected cups of coffee and then retreated into Dr Daly's room.

'I've sat on a number of Parole Boards. I always dread hearing on the news that someone we've released has committed another serious offence.'

'I'm not a member of a Board as such, so I won't be burdened in quite the way you have been. I exist to be a sort of go-between, getting to know applicants, staff and above all the victims and their families, drawing these things together and making a recommendation which of course the Board are totally free to reject.'

'But they won't. It was very rare indeed for us not to be directed by the sort of reports you are talking about. Your particular role is new to me, but I suspect it will be the one listened to most attentively.'

'Oh dear. That's what I feared.'

'So what do you think happened on your way back from there?'

'It obviously wasn't anything physical, and they were extremely thorough in the A&E department.'

The doctor turned to his computer and looked the screen over.

'Yes. There was nothing abnormal detected, which is why you've been sent to me, I suppose. But the paramedics' report is clear that you were unconscious when they got to you, so something happened of significance. So, let me ask again, what do you think happened?'

Alex stayed silent for a while.

'My life has taken some unusual turns in the past few years. Iris Murdoch could probably have made a novel from them, well she could if she was still alive.'

'Yes, and I'm aware of some of those turns and twists. For example you're the first person I've ever met to have died in a plane crash!'

'Don't remind me. At least I didn't see the news here or any of the reports in the papers. Thank goodness for the heavy Sunday evening traffic in Seattle. It saved our lives. We had checked in before we set off for the airport, so our names were on the manifest produced after the crash, which is why we were said to have been amongst the dead, but we missed the flight and when the crash occurred we were on a bus.'

'There is a well-established condition known as Survivor Syndrome, or Survivor Guilt.'

'I've heard of it but whether my panic attack had anything to do with that I just can't say. It would be mere speculation. Have you an alternative to offer me?'

Dr Daly laughed.

'Multiple Choice, you mean?'

'Whatever.'

'I don't think we're looking for an alternative as such, so much as something that accompanied it: delayed Post Traumatic Stress Disorder following your almost miraculous escape from death. I can't be certain because we don't yet have the psychiatric equivalent of a scanner that can read what is happening in your brain, but you had just had another shock, that of going into a high-security prison and encountering wicked people. Prisons are not pleasant places and I sometimes have to go to Wakefield to do an assessment and I can't wait to get out again afterwards.

'However, I feel certain that the event on the train was a combination of three circumstances: your day in Banklyn, Survivor Syndrome and PTSD. It may never happen again but I think you should exercise a watching brief. I would not recommend any kind of talking therapy, so called.'

'I wasn't thinking of it, but why do you say that?'

'Primarily because I think you have no need of it. I'm sure it can help some people, though often at great expense, but your life experience so far, which is to say the least colourful, would have any therapist salivating in anticipation. I would urge you to stay away from it because all I think it would do would be to screw you up.'

'I do have a concern which with your experience you might be able to help. It's not a hypothetical question and I'm unsure whether I will be infringing the Official Secrets Act in telling you, but I imagine you also are bound by that Act.'

'I am certainly but if it concerns a prisoner who has applied for parole, it would be entirely inappropriate for me to hear about it just in case someone drops out and I am asked to deputise. It has happened before.'

'No it doesn't .'

Alex spelled-out the story told to him by Angus, the prison chaplain and his fear or concern that illegal substances were entering the prison via the governor.'

The doctor did not speak for a while.

'Drugs getting into prison has become a major issue,' he said. 'A lot of the people I see have either begun taking drugs inside or have done little other inside than take drugs, and many are emerging with serious difficulties because of it in terms both of their mental health and also major financial difficulties caused by the suppliers charging families a lot of money with menaces. It would be nice to say there is a subculture of drug taking in our prisons, but what we are talking about is much bigger than that. The problem in a place like Banklyn and why there is extra security in place is because most of those men are there for a very long time. No doubt taking drugs eases life in the pit in which they live but if it leads to even more serious mental states than those that took them in there in the first place, we are all in trouble and especially if they apply for parole. Keeping drugs out is essential.

'The chaplain is in an unenviable position. If drugs are getting in and if it is true that the supplier is holding the highest office in the place, the chaplain needs to watch his step if he reveals this knowledge. The men who run this kind of operation are ruthless and I'm not exaggerating when I say they are quite prepared to kill anyone who gets in their way. And if it's true that the governor is involved, it will be because they have a tight hold of him or someone in his near circle. You, Alex, must not be any further involved. The work of the chaplain is outside your remit in relation to the Parole Board, and you mustn't compromise the work you are there to do. You have a wife and two children to think about and it is vital that you have no further involvement or contact with the chaplain. I cannot stress this enough.'

Chapter Twelve

As Alex drove home all he could hear in his head was the echo of Dr Daly's words of warning, words which he knew he meant. The prospect of someone hurting a member of his family as a warning to him was too much to bear and part of him, even now as the Parole process was drawing to a close, wanted to have nothing more to do with it. Yet, he was anxious also about Angus and he desperately hoped that having been warned off by his boss, he was keeping to that.

The appointment with the psychiatrist had really been much ado about nothing as he had anticipated, though he had been helpful in one or two matters regarding the Parole Board report he would have to be writing once he had done his final visit to Branklyn. He therefore decided that he would telephone the governor today and arrange to meet the five members of staff selected by him within a couple of days. Would he also want to see Armstrong for a final time? He couldn't think of a reason why and certainly not to wish him well.

He was in good time to collect Chloe and George from Fiona, their childminder. He recalled her mother, his former secretary on the National Park Committee, saying that she was something of a looker, and he had to admit that she was quite right, so going to collect the children was not a great hardship, which was precisely not the sort of thought a priest or bishop should be having, so thankfully he was now neither.

He called in at home for a cup of coffee and checking his emails found that a date had been fixed for the Board to meet. He was not required to be there but his report needed to be in soon, which provided him with exactly the leverage he intended to use with the governor for his final visit.

Fiona had five children with her this morning – perhaps she doubled up as Wonder Woman in her spare time – and gave a full report on how Chloe and George had been during the morning, but did say that neither had slept and that it was therefore likely that they would sleep in the car on their way home. They did and Alex had to wake them for lunch about which they were unimpressed.

Emily was having a day out, visiting a school in Sheffield as the recently-appointed City Laureate. For the first time some of her poems had been included on the syllabus for English A-level and so from across the city came keen young people to work with her for a day. It was the second time she had done this and if it was anything like the first time, she would be enjoying herself enormously.

Once he had finished lunch with the children and changed their nappies and put them down to play, but before he had had the chance to wash up, which included washing not only plates and cutlery but the chairs themselves and of course the floor, he had a phone call from Amy.

'So, how did it go?'

'Okay. Nothing special and to be perfectly honest I learnt nothing new other than a few tips on preparing my report for the Parole Board.'

Did he mention anything about therapy or spiritual direction?'

'Certainly not the latter, but he did strongly advise me against any sort of talking therapy.'

'And will you be seeing him again?'

'He didn't mention it and I can't see how or why I would need to do so.'

'Well, that's good, and how are my grandchildren today?'

'I think they're in good form. When will they see you again?'

'Oh later. I called in this morning while you were both out and I picked up a huge pile of things requiring ironing with which I've been occupying myself, so I'll drop it round when Emily's back.'

The children were still at the stage of needing an after lunch sleep and having had only a truncated nap earlier did not take long to settle, allowing Alex to phone the governor and arrange his final visit in the following week.

'By the way,' said Andy, 'have you had any chance to mull over our conversation about Angus Smallwood?'

'No. It wouldn't be right for me to make any comment. I don't have any appropriate experience to know how he is doing. My task is simply to help the Board reach a decision, beyond that I am not allowed to tread.'

'Thank you all the same for listening to me yesterday, and I'll look forward to seeing you next week for the final time.'

'Until the next time.'

'Ah yes, I was forgetting that you are our permanent PB liaison officer.'

Adolescent boys always found Emily compelling and Alex could well understand why, because he felt exactly the same. Even after twins she was utterly gorgeous and possessed astonishing intelligence and maturity. She was proving to be an equally brilliant poet and her latest collection had been universally well received.

Arriving home from her day in Sheffield she was animated as she told Alex all about it, and not least the two 17-year-olds she had singled out for particular attention.

'Boys, I take it?'

'Yes.'

'Darling, they fall in love with you and super-charged with testosterone they will fancy you like mad, as I do. You know this.'

'Of course I do, and I love it, but you must tell me about your morning which is much more important than my lovely young men.'

'There's little to tell. He felt I might have a measure of PTSD and Survivor Guilt from our air crash brought on by my visit to Branklyn, He advised me against any sort of talking therapy. He was a nice man and he gave me one or two insights into how I should complete my report for the Parole Board. That was it.'

Not for the first time, Paul, whose real name was Norman, and his boss, met for lunch in The Old George in Goole, where they knew they could rely on receiving good food.

'So how are your Monday mornings going?'

'Can't complain. She's a nice lady and we get on well.'

'How does your girlfriend feel about it?'

'Least said the better.'

'You don't feel Linda is a liability?'

'No, besides which she is now so totally compromised handling the stuff and passing on the reward to her son and his wife, that she knows she could say nothing even if I was to pull out – if you will excuse my expression.'

The man laughed.

'But what about the man on the inside, her husband, is he solid?' asked Norman.

'Oh yes. Like her he's utterly and completely compromised, I'm pleased to say. He would be staring at a very long stretch if everything goes tits up, and he knows it. However we do have one little fly in the ointment which I think you could probably help us with. It's called the Reverend Angus Smallwood and he's the prison chaplain and from what he has said, we think it's quite possible that he suspects something is amiss on the drugs front, and that he may even have worked out how the stuff is getting in there. It may be that he has, as yet, told no one else about this, not least because he is bound by the Official Secrets Act, and we very much like matters to stay just like that, with him saying nothing.

'He's a bachelor which almost certainly in the church means he's queer, and one possibility would be for him to be arrested for indecency which would completely rule out any possibility that he returns to his work. But he might then take the opportunity of squealing, which on the whole we don't think would be a good thing for us. So, I immediately thought of you. I don't actually give a shit whether he dies or not. After all if he does he'll no doubt go straight to heaven, but I think he needs some encouragement to keep his mouth firmly and permanently shut, if you take my meaning.'

'No problem. Just let me have the details and I'll see to it.'

He handed over some pieces of paper which Norman put away at once.

'There will be a nice bonus in this. You could take Linda away for a night to a very posh hotel.'

'I think I'd rather take Felicity if you don't mind. With old ladies I have to work twice as hard.'

The man laughed.

'One other thing, Norman. At the bottom of those papers is a phone number and would you be able to find out whether Smallwood has been in the habit of calling it? It's a number somewhere in Derbyshire, and if he has been calling it, we may need to extend the area of your operation.'

'That'll be straightforward.'

'Good man, let me get in the same again.'

Paul rummaged out his mobile and speed dialled an acquaintance.

'How are you doing, Tolly. It's Paul here. I've got a nice little earner for you if you're interested. 500. Yeah. Ok, I'll call round in about an hour.'

'Setting something up already?' asked the man as he put onto the table his own pint and Paul's St Clement's.'

'I'm sure you really don't want to know,' Norman replied with a grin.

Whatever else Teddy Armstrong might be, stupid he was not. His application for parole had been long in the planning though that had not included the interference of Alex Elliot who had so riled him at their last meeting that for a short time he had quite lost his cool. The ex-Bishop was planning another visit which would not include himself though he could always ask the governor if Elliot would be willing to see him. He was hoping that his brief at the Board would try to make null and void anything that came from the parents by virtue of presenting to the members of the Board the vile letters he had received from them. And then there was the matter of the governor.

The fact of drugs now being easily available in Branklyn was common knowledge to the permanent residents and by now probably also to the majority of the screws, and the rumour was that even some of them were obtaining and using. Teddy being a good observer of life in the institution thought there must be at least two people involved, someone bringing in the merchandise and someone inside distributing it. Giving it a lot of thought and applying the methodology of Sherlock Holmes: "Once you eliminate the impossible, whatever remains, no matter how improbable, must be the truth." This answer could hardly be more improbable, he thought, because he now believed that the importer was none other than the governor himself, not least because he was not searched and sniffed like everyone else first thing in the morning. Of course neither was Myles Hammond, his deputy, but Teddy ruled him out completely. Earlier he had been informed of the date of his coming Board which was music to Teddy's ears and so he put in a request to see the governor urgently, and was told they could meet later that afternoon, an arrangement which suited Teddy ideally.

Angus Smallwood was taking a few days off from work. He went and did some gardening before coming in and reading, in the process of which he fell fast asleep. He knew that he ought to go and pay a visit to an ancient aunt living in Burton upon Trent, but today he felt just too idle, so instead would call her and indicate that he might well see her tomorrow.

Away from the prison he rarely thought about the place and his captive audience, though few attended Sunday worship and of those who did, even fewer paid attention to his words, including, he had to admit, himself.

At the back of his mind was the thought that he might seek to make contact with Alex Elliot, and possibly meet well away from the prison, but he also realised that this would compromise Elliot and possibly render his work on the Parole application of Teddy Armstrong null and void. All the same he recognised Elliot to be a source of wisdom, so perhaps after the Board had taken place it could be arranged.

Much to her delight, Emily received a call from Peter Cheeseman saying that if the offer was still open, might there be the chance of his coming to stay for just a couple of nights this coming weekend as he would be on his way to a diocesan conference to be held in nearby Swanwick?

'Peter, that would be wonderful. If you're coming by train

we'll arrange to meet you at Sheffield station. Will there just be you?'

'Yes,'

'By the way, when you come please call him Alex. He would wish you to do so.'

'Ok, but it won't be easy. And, at the risk of embarrassing you, may I say that when we met in Windermere for a brief moment I thought you were that woman off *Countryfile*, Ellie Harrison.'

'I will accept the compliment.'

If Teddy had been thought of as a loner in Pooley Bridge, it had been very much the same in both Wakefield and here. Only rarely did he take advantage of Association to have contact with his fellow inmates other than at mealtimes. His cell door was therefore already unlocked when one of the screws came to collect him for his interview with the governor that he had requested.

Andy sat behind his desk and Teddy was made to stand in front of it. The screw who had brought him remained in the room by the door. Teddy deliberately looked round at him and then back towards Andy.

'I thought that as this concerns my application for Parole, we should operate on a one-to-one basis, not in the presence of another who just might have to be interviewed by the liaison officer on his next and final visit.'

Teddy smiled cynically.

Andy sighed audibly.

'Mr Welby, perhaps you could wait on the other side of that door.'

Once they were alone, and without being invited, Teddy pulled up a chair and sat down.

'It won't have escaped your attention,' he said, 'that I wish to be released from prison. I've served my time and I know what I did was very wrong indeed, but my hope is that I can live as normal a life as possible for as long as it lasts, and that means outside. The Parole Board meets soon and much will depend upon your report, that from the medics and the report produced by the liaison officer. The Board must by now be well used to the sorts of things spoken of by the victims which, understandably, will always be detrimental to the chances of parole and I'm pretty sure that will be the same in my own case.

'I very much hope that in your own report you will say that I have been a model prisoner, because I have in every way and I have every intention of being a model citizen when I get out – and I hope you will say that too. I did things that were heinous and there would be no shortage of people in our society willing to tear me limb from limb but because we are a relatively civilised society, our justice system allows alternatives.

In coming to see you, Governor, I want to convince you that getting rid of me would be advantageous for us both. It's not long now until your Prison Inspectorate Visitation, something I know you think is very important and of course, is. I honestly believe that happening will be more straightforward without my presence. After all it would not be good news if it was discovered that the recent proliferation of magic bullets in the place was brought about by someone in high office – if you take my meaning.'

'Do you know the range of sentences available to the judge when attempting blackmail?'

'Nice try, Governor. Anyway I'll leave it with you for the present. It'll give you something to chew over on your way home and just might help you as you set about writing your report for the Parole Board.'

'If you were released, there would be nothing to stop you repeating these ridiculous allegations to the press.'

'Trust me, Andy, when I am released I will never give thought to this place again!'

He stood, pushed back the chair and walked towards the door, not looking back.

Andy sat there a while before he picked up his phone, speed dialled a number and simply said, 'We need to meet.'

Chapter Thirteen

Alex was determined to make his final visit to Brantlyn as brief as possible. He was realistic enough to know that the five prison officers chosen by the governor would have absolutely nothing controversial or even interesting to say, and would reflect the governor's own views about Armstrong. Amy had agreed to take the children to the childminder and for once, Alex decided to drive to the prison. He had been sent a pass for parking at the beginning of his time there but not used it until today. Bearing in mind all that Dr Daly had told him, it was essential to avoid the chaplain.

The one thing he would miss from his visits to prison was the excited attention of the sniffing spaniels. Their handlers too were also quite unlike the other officers and seemed to have caught from their charges something of the joy of life, in which everything was a game. Once he had completed the security process, he received his keys and descended the circles of hell, which as a lover of Dante he liked to think of them being such, though more prosaically he had to go upstairs!'

Having come by car he arrived at an unusual time for him and the governor's office was empty, probably because he was on his rounds, so he admitted himself and went to the corner of the room and sat in an armchair and took out from his bag a book for it was and had been for many years his usual practice of carrying about with him reading material for use in any gap the day might generously provide. He was still reading Jeremy Taylor on "Holy Dying".

He heard the door opening and expected it to be Andy, but when he looked he saw only a prison officer he recognised but couldn't name, who was going through the large briefcase that was already open and standing on a chair by the door. It was clear to Alex that he was removing some items and transferring them to a sort of rucksack he was carrying. Alex watched until the man had clearly finished, and then said, 'Good morning.'

The man who didn't look particularly fit, almost died of shock.

'Er, er, hello, sir.'

'Have you managed to get what you need?'

'Er, yes. The governor generously brings me in certain kinds of dog food. We've both got labradors and we often share ideas about food.'

'That's good. I should think that feeding a labrador is quite an expensive business.'

'It is, but they're such wonderful companions.'

Andy himself now came into the room.

'I was just chatting with Dr Elliot, sir, but I'll be off.'

He closed the door and left his rucksack.

'I didn't know you were a dog man.'

'In which case you were correct, I'm not, though my wife, Linda, would love to get a labrador. Well now, this is your final visit regarding Armstrong, though there will be others in time. I asked Myles to select the five officers for you to talk to, just in case you thought I would only choose those who would reflect my views.'

'I don't know you well Andy, but I would never expect that of you. You haven't got to where you are now in the prison service without maintaining total integrity.'

'Thank you Alex. That's very kind. On a different and very serious matter, I take it you will have heard the terrible news about our chaplain, Angus Smallwood.'

Alex's face became suddenly very serious.

'No.'

'Two nights ago he came out of a club in Hull, one apparently that he frequented along with other gay men, and as he was opening his car, presumably to return home, witnesses say he was approached by a young black person who may have been after his wallet. Apparently Angus tried to push him away and get into his car when the young man produced a knife, stabbed him several times and took his wallet with him as he rapidly departed.'

'Oh my God. Is he in hospital?'

'I'm afraid to say that if he is, it will be in the mortuary. He was pronounced dead on arrival.'

'Jesus – that's terrible.'

'It is, but what makes me feel even worse is that I had a conversation with you about my anxieties about him.'

'Yes, I can imagine how that makes you feel, but it doesn't sound like it was you outside a gay club in Hull, blacked up and wielding a knife. The world is meant to be different now and all supposed to be accepting of diversity but I guess that if you go to a club such as that you easily make yourself a target for the prejudices of others. Do you know anything at all about the funeral arrangements?'

'Nothing other than that he had no immediate family and the Bishop of Hull has said he will make all the necessary arrangements. I imagine you will know better than me how to get that information.'

'If the Bishop of Hull takes the funeral Angus will be spinning in his coffin before he gets anywhere near his grave! They didn't see eye to eye.'

Alex paid little attention to anything the five prison officers said to him in answer to his pre-prepared questions. The only thing on his mind was what had happened to Angus Smallwood and wondering what he should now do about it. Tony Daly's warning now assumed monumental proportions, and thinking about Emily, Chloe, George and Amy he instinctively felt he must protect them and if that therefore meant doing nothing about what he knew from Angus, surely that just might have to be. Or was he choosing to allow evil to flourish?

He knew that he allowed evil to flourish all the time across the face of the earth, about which he did nothing, but about which he could do nothing. To do something about this risked bringing harm on those whom he most loved, and possibly even more than harm. Yet he had seen for himself this morning proof of the very claim that Angus had spoken of, that the person bringing drugs into the prison was the governor himself and he also knew the face of the inside man distributing them.

The Bluebell was quiet at this time of the early evening so there seemed little chance of any conversation being overheard.

'It's good to see you Andy, and I hear that all is well with Karl, Joan and the children, which must be a source of great relief to you. I don't really understand why our grown-up kids feel the need to conceal from us the difficult bad things in their lives, but you've made a significant difference to theirs.'

'It's taken a great weight off our minds, I can tell you.'

'When we started your wife had considerable anxieties about it all. How does she feel now?'

'We hardly ever talk about it – it's just become an ordinary part of our life.'

'And I was very sorry to hear about the terrible thing that happened to your chaplain. I assume they will replace him, but let's hope it's a married man who won't take the sort of silly risks your man took visiting clubs. I'm told that the church is awash with poofs so heaven alone knows (if you will forgive my expression) what you'll get next, perhaps even a woman.'

'I'm not sure that would be a good thing given the offenders we've got in there.'

'Fair point. But on this occasion I take it you have something on your mind that perhaps I might help with.'

'He's called Teddy Armstrong and 21 years ago he abducted and raped and murdered two sisters, aged 6 and 8. The ridiculous judge sentenced him to life imprisonment – but said he could be considered for parole after 20 years. Even now I can't believe the judge said that, as it should have been 30 years minimum. Now he has applied for parole and therefore the Parole Board has set in motion the process whereby his appeal will be considered. Speaking off the record, I personally would have strung him up as I think any reasonably minded person would if they had read the complete trial transcript. He's a vile disgusting human being, and doesn't deserve to live. In prison he is highly manipulative but has earned a degree from the OU in computer studies. He is almost always totally in control of himself and says that what he did was evil and that he even wishes he were dead to spare him the memory. It's what will impress the Board and echoed, I'm sure, by the psychos who have examined him and will report on him. The only person he could not convince is the Liaison Officer who also has a report to give.'

'Is he the one you mentioned previously that you thought your chaplain might have been in touch with?'

'Yes.'

'You can put your mind rest on that. There was no contact between the two.'

'I'm pleased about that as he's a good man. Armstrong is not, and he has somehow or other, probably through observation and the use of his intelligence, worked out who it is that is bringing contraband into the place.'

'That's not so good.'

'With that knowledge he is demanding that I write a report recommending his release.'

'Are you able to do that?'

'Do I have any choice?'

'You mean he's got you over a barrel. If he's not released, he has the information; if they release him, he might still want to use that information .'

'Exactly.'

'This Board thing, when is it due to take place?'

'In two weeks' time.'

'What would your preference be? Once he is out, we can easily persuade him to say nothing but if the Board does not accept his application we would need to find a way of maintaining his silence inside. After all it's important that you are not damaged. It could happen before the Board meets if you thought that the best way of resolving the issue.'

'But how would you manage that?'

'We have done it elsewhere, and you could leave it to us.'

'All things considered it wouldn't be good news for me if something happened to him before the Board met. Afterwards would probably be best, either way.'

'I think you're probably right.'

Once the children were in bed, Emily and Alex had some supper.

'Alex, tell me, regardless of any state secrets you may convey, what has happened today, because something has? I could tell from the moment you got back.'

'It's not a secret and although it didn't happen today, I only learned about it when I was at the prison this morning. It's Angus, the prison chaplain with whom I've spoken twice. He was murdered, stabbed, coming out of a club late at night. I looked up the Hull Daily Mail on the Internet when I got back. All it said was that police were looking for a black youth but I got the impression, reading between the lines, that they weren't exactly doing so assiduously. I suspect the police would not regard a gay man as much of a priority.'

'Alex, that's terrible.'

'It gets worse, my love. Whilst I was waiting in the governor's office for him to return from doing his rounds, I watched a prison officer come in – he didn't see me – and remove from an open briefcase certain items which he then placed into a bag he was carrying. I'm certain that what he was removing was a consignment of drugs, and that they were brought in by the governor himself, which is what Angus believed was going on.'

'My darling, there is no way you can be involved any further. You have now completed all your visits and need not go there again. Your report will go to London and has only one concern, not anything to do with the running of the prison by any of its staff. If that can happen to Angus, it could take you from us. Surely you see that.'

'There's no doubt that Dr Daly would agree with you 100%, because that is exactly what he told me when I told him what Angus had discovered. I suspect he's had more, much more involvement with nasty people in the course of his work and he was adamant in what he said.'

'Then you must take notice of him, even if you take no notice of me.'

'In this world the person I take most notice of is you in just about every situation, closely followed by your mother. Please understand I would do nothing to place you, the children, Amy or myself in any danger, but a murder has been committed, the murder of a priest, the murder of a human being. To do nothing would be to commit the sin of omission, failing to do what is right. What is open for me to do I have no idea but I can promise you that there is no way in which I will act without first having talked it over with you and Amy.'

'Perhaps you can talk it over with Peter Cheeseman because, and I forgot to tell you, he's coming to stay here at the weekend. Apparently your successor in Truro, your former assistant bishop, Colin Morris, has his heart set on doing something relevant by which he means a diocesan conference, though in my experience you only have a conference when you have no intention of doing anything else. It's a great substitute for action.'

Alex laughed.

'Is Peter coming unaccompanied?'

'Apparently lovers, mistresses and ladies of the night are not welcome at Swanwick.'

'I can well imagine but I'm glad he's coming because he might just be the right person to help me unravel the knot this has all brought about. I need therefore give tomorrow morning and evening over to writing the report and sending it off.'

'Do they trust such important documents to the postal services?'

'Oh no. It's done making use of a series of passwords. It will be a little like playing table tennis. I send a covering letter referring to known persons with a password, and they reply using another password, and only then can I send my report, using a third password. It's supposed to protect security and not least because the passwords change each week.'

'Tomorrow I'll stop work at lunchtime and allow you the afternoon to complete what you're doing unless, you're expecting Chloe and George contributing.'

'Perhaps I will finish before lunch. If so, why do we not take the children out in their buggy for a country walk.'

'That's a wonderful idea but only if you have finished. And don't worry about my writing. I was trying to write a poem about daffodils but I just can't get out of my mind the thought someone just might have done it already though I can't think who!'

'Oh, bad luck. Perhaps you could instead write one about a flea that bites us both and mingles our blood inside itself.'

'Nice try, but I think it's been done – sorry about the pun!'

Alex rose early, made some tea (it was too early for Emily, and the children were still both asleep in the bed with mummy). He looked over for the hundredth time the instructions which insisted that no more than 750 words would be accepted and began his first draft. At breakfast time he stopped and after that he drove the children to Fiona's. He now had over two hours before he need collect them and he wanted to maximise the time so his heart sank when George wanted him to stay. Normally he would have welcomed the chance to stay with the children and especially with the lovely Fiona, but this morning George demanded that daddy stayed and only stopped crying when daddy was in sight. After an hour Fiona announced that because it was such a lovely day they would all go outside in their buggies. Whether this was because Fiona sensed that Alex needed to be somewhere else he didn't know, but it was a perfect time to make his escape and Fiona and her two assistants began dressing the children. George loved being outside and so hadn't notice daddy slip away.

Emily was outside waiting for Alex to arrive back.'

'Fiona telephoned and George is very unsettled. I gather he wouldn't let you go and then when they got back from their outing and found you gone, he started again. Fiona's taken his temperature, and it's high but not too bad, so I'll bring them both back here. If need be, I can take him to the doctor.'

'Ok,' said Alex, handing over the car keys. In a moment Emily was on her way.

Alex went to his desk and sat down, turning on his mac and going to where he had left off earlier. Outside it was now raining and, unusually, he felt sad, not for himself, but above all for Angus and he wondered whether he had failed him by not doing something, even if he could not have known what that might be. He looked at the screen and there emblazoned across the top of the page were the two words: Theodore Armstrong.

Ironically, after all the interruptions and false starts of the morning, the words came easily, suggesting that a lot of his thinking, like all good thinking, had been taking place unconsciously. He detailed his visits and conversations and concluded that he could not recommend parole for the prisoner primarily because he was engaging in a charade of being reformed and quiet, just wanting to live out the rest of his life ever conscious of the terrible he had once done. Alex concluded that he was wholly unconvinced by Armstrong and that the parents of his victims were also his victims and continued to bear the scars of his heinous acts.

So engrossed was he in this that he did not hear the arrival home of Emily and the children and it was only the sound of her voice as she sat with them reading a story that brought him back into the land of the living. He rose from his chair and went out to them.

'Hello, little ones, all three of you!' he said and received three warm smiles in return as his reward.

'How's George?'

'I think he may have a slight ear infection as he keeps putting his hand there. Fiona said he had a slight temperature but nothing to worry about. It's quite common in small children but it can hurt, so I'll give him some Calpol and he might manage some sleep after lunch. How are you getting on?'

'Finished, apart from tidying up, and I shall be glad to be shot of it, I can tell you, and I'm not at all sure I want to do another one, but I'm sorry it's messed up your morning.'

'It hasn't, honestly, but if you look on my desk, you'll see that I've had some hate mail, presumably from the same people who interrupted me at Hay. One of them however, is from a former English don at Oxford whose academic work has usually been really good. In retirement she has apparently become a member of an extreme left-wing group and has decided that I'm a total traitor and says she will do all she can to deter people reading me.'

'How many in her left-wing alliance would read you, anyway?'

'And I wonder just how many of her comrades know she is the owner of two large houses, one in Oxford and the other in South Wales?'

The children were getting bored with the conversation between their parents and begged Emily to return to the much more important matter in hand featuring the diet of the Hungry Caterpillar!

When the phone had rung earlier, Emily had been in the heaven she enjoyed whenever Alex was not around: the wonderful world of John Donne and she could hardly believe her good fortune that Nicky was commissioning a book from her on her favourite subject. When she and Alex had got together in the US she had wondered if Donne was just a substitute for real love with a real man and would fade in her affections, but it wasn't so, and quite the opposite was true in that the love poems she had always gloried in meant more not less now that she and her wonderful man shared their bed together, and although she had not told him yet (and when would that be, she wondered?), now she was with Alex, even Donne's religious poems had begun to mean a lot more to her. Alex would smile.

Nicky had set her a deadline, but it was still some time off (though Nicky's deadlines were serious) so she could still luxuriate in his heart and mind. It also gave her a break from the different mental activity of creating poetry, the poetry that raised the ire of the left.

On the following evening the phone rang and Emily answered it as Alex was in the kitchen preparing supper. It was a call from Dr Daly, the psychiatrist that Alex had visited. She called him.

'Dr Daly,' said Alex, 'this is a surprise. Don't tell me you were looking at the wrong brain scan and have now discovered I haven't got one.'

'Believe me, we all have one. How we use it is what matters. But look Alex, the reason I'm calling is that I have just received word from a priest I know in Hull that the chaplain of Brantlyn of whom you and I have spoken, has been murdered outside a nightclub mostly frequented by gay men. I rang a colleague at the hospital there and he told me that although the police were engaged in finding the perpetrator, at best their efforts could be described as perfunctory. The thought seems to be that gay men alone in the middle of the night are almost asking for it.'

'Yes, I'm afraid I heard something similar when I was at the prison the other day. I wasn't aware of tears being shed.'

'Prison officers are not on the whole known for their advanced social views, many of them being further to the right than Attila the Hun. But I'm ringing you now to underline what I said when we met, if not for your own sake, then for your wife's and childrens' sake, don't get involved.'

'You would be of the opinion that his murder was wholly intentional and had to do with what he seems to have discovered at Brantlyn?'

'I have no doubt for one moment. Remember Alex, you're in the world of serious crime. It is an amoral world in which life is held cheap, and it wouldn't matter in the slightest to them that you have held high and responsible positions. If they felt it right and that you were endangering the accumulation of money and power, they would have no compunction in killing you. Whoever is running all this would not do it themselves, but the promise of money and drugs will induce others to do so.'

'You make it sound a very scary world.'

'That's because it is, but Alex, I very much would like you, and your family, to pop down the motorway to Nottingham, to have lunch with me. There are a couple of things I would like you to see, important things to me but they might just resonate in you too.'

'That sounds most intriguing. Yes is the answer. I'll consult the oracle and get back to you, if that's okay.'

'Saturday would be the best day for me, but just let me know when it might be possible. In the meantime, well you know what I will say: be very careful.'

Chapter Fourteen

Peter's train was due in at 3.45 though as he sat on the platform, Alex knew it was highly unlikely to be on-time and so it was no surprise at all when it finally turned up at 4.15. He hadn't minded because as always, he had brought a book with him and despite the hurly-burly of station comings and goings he was able to switch it all off and concentrate on his reading. It was a gift for which he was grateful and it had been like had ever since he was a child, much to the frustration of his mother calling him to the meal table. His parents had divorced not long after he had been born and although he saw his father occasionally, it was left to his mother to bring him up. There was no money to have him privately educated and he went to the local comprehensive where he shone academically and was utterly useless on the sports field. That was fortunate for Alex as it meant he was not required to surrender his Saturdays to team games, but could stay at home and read. Considering what he later became, albeit for only a short while, there was no religion or the hint of it, in his upbringing. He was devastated when his mother died, being so very close to her. She had never been a smoker and yet is one of those unlucky people who nevertheless contracted lung cancer and, as is so very often the case, it wasn't diagnosed until too late. Even now, a good many years on, his eyes could fill with tears at his memory of her, and how he wished she could have known her grandchildren. She would however have howled with laughter at the thought he had been a bishop of the Church of England. Come to think of it, he often howled with laughter at the thought himself.

The train pulled into the station and moments later Alex spotted Peter and they waved to one another. Alex went to help him with his luggage and they gave each other a welcoming hug.

'Emily says I have to call you Alex. Is that really alright?'

'I rather think so, otherwise i might have to call you Reverend Cheeseman!'

'Heaven forfend!'

They both laughed and walked to the car park.

'Do tell me what it is you're supposed to be doing at Swanwick next week?' asked Alex once they had passed through the worst of the early evening traffic.

'It's something we have been told that is very important and rooted in theology: new ways of financing the church.'

'That's quite funny. Now tell me the truth.'

'I'm sorry Alex, but it is the truth, and I'm far from convinced it's going to be very funny.'

'It makes my heart sink and doubles my rejoicing that I'm free of it. And is that everything?'

'There are various workshops and we all have to sign up for at least two. There's also lowest common denominator worship and Bible study each morning given by the suffragan Bishop of Hume in the diocese of Manchester.'

'And is attendance compulsory?'

'It is unless you write a note to the Bishop explaining that you've got a cold and won't be doing cross country either.'

Alex grinned. Having Peter around for the weekend was going to be fun.

From the moment he arrived the children adored Peter and it was abundantly clear that he was a total natural with them, feeding them at teatime, helping with their bath and reading them a bedtime story which still they couldn't understand but loved.

Downstairs Alex was waiting with a G&T which unquestionably Peter had earned. Over supper Emily asked him whether he would be interested at some stage in having children, now that it was possible for gay couples.

'The answer is yes and no. I love children and on a Sunday morning I would much rather be in the Sunday school than in church. They are wholly nonjudgemental and tell it exactly how it is. I fear most adults have lost that combination. Anyway one of the things I wanted to tell you, or more realistically ask your thoughts about, is a change of job. I'm thinking of applying to be the warden of a hostel for women needing a halfway house between prison and a return to whatever passes for normal life. The odd thing about the job specification is that they deliberately want a man to do it, otherwise these girls and women would have no contact with a man.'

'I would think you are ideally suited for such a job,' said Alex, 'the first requirement of which would be infinite compassion and a rich sense of humour. I'm no guide nor a career adviser, but I think you should give it a go. You've got nothing to lose and possibly everything to gain.

'A former Archbishop of Canterbury, although at the time just a diocesan bishop, was reliably informed that one of his clergy had become attached to a married lady in his parish, bringing about the break-up of her marriage. Quite rightly the priest was suspended. Being a forgiving soul he offered him alternative employment, and believe it or not he became the chaplain of a boarding school for girls. Perhaps he should have been given another chance, but perhaps that was not the wisest choice.'

'You would know only too well, Alex, but the life of a

diocesan bishop must be made up of many trials and getting it right can't always be easy.'

'Well I only did it for a very short while and it really wasn't for me, but this job sounds as if it could be ideal for you, Peter. Whereabouts is it?'

'On the edge of Bristol.'

'It might be helpful to your application if you are able to become familiar with the world of street drugs, as I imagine many of those young women going into prison and coming out of prison will have major problems in that area, and I very much hope it doesn't rain in the morning, because I need to talk through with you and seek your wisdom on a matter not unrelated to that.'

Peter looked up at Emily.

'It's lovely to be here and to be so near such a gifted poet and a man I admire so very much.'

'Peter, we are delighted that you are able to be here.'

There was wind but no rain as Alex and Peter set out after breakfast, despite complaints from Chloe and George that daddy was taking Peter away from them. At first they chatted about the countryside, it being the one thing Peter knew he would miss if he were appointed in Bristol. Then Alex decided to unburden himself and let Peter know as much of the story as he could without compromising himself in terms of the Official Secrets Act, though eventually found it so difficult to do so, he decided to risk it and tell him all.

As he recounted the events of his involvement at the prison (omitting all mention of Armstrong and the parents of his victims) Peter did not interrupt once, not even when Alex reported the murder of Angus in Hull. When he had finished they walked on in silence for almost a quarter of a mile before Peter spoke.

'If you chose to expose all that was going on, and believe me I'm not suggesting that as a course of action, how would you do it?'

'I suppose I would simultaneously inform the Ministry of Justice via the Cabinet Office, and the police.'

'And as far as you know the chaplain had not done that himself?'

'As far as I know, but I have grave suspicions about how institutions function having worked in two of them at a high level. It is by no means unknown for them to let sleeping dogs lie rather than face the fuss that might be generated if they are awakened. You see, I don't know whether the officials overseeing the prisons are now so resigned to the presence of drugs on such a large-scale, that they feel they could do nothing about it. If that is the case then possibly those sleeping dogs will continue to lie there and someone like me given the order of the boot.'

'But someone's been murdered. Surely that can't be allowed to pass unnoticed?'

'It's pretty clear that the efforts of the police are somewhat perfunctory, the reason for that being that he was gay and coming out from a club, and presumably therefore asking for it.'

'Your psychiatrist friend, who sounds as if he has had a lot of experience with unpleasant people, has told you to steer well clear, not least because of Emily, Chloe and George. Don't you think that's advice well worth heeding?'

'I do. Very much indeed. It's just whether I should nevertheless do something. You will, I'm sure, know the traditional syllogism: "I must do something; this is something; I must do this". I don't care about the drugs in prison and, who knows, if I was sentenced to life in prison I might long for them to deaden the pain. But I do care about Angus.'

'Alex this is a lovely walk. Thank you for bringing me and

indeed thank you for letting me come to be with you and Emily. What I do need is some time to think about what you've said. It deserves considerably more than a hasty response and one thing I do know about myself is that I do my best thinking when I'm not thinking. Sorry that probably sounds ridiculous, but it's how I function. If I sit down to write a sermon I know full well it will be crap, but if I stop thinking about it completely and then preach, I know it'll be okay. Perhaps what you need me to do is to go into Sheffield and watch whichever team is playing at home this afternoon, then possibly I might have something to say.'

'If you were to do that, is there any chance at all that you'd be willing to take Emily with you? She is always saying she would love to go to a football match, not so much because of the game, but more because of the ambience.'

'I'm told that the former Bishop of Southwark, Mervyn Stockwood, a character if ever there was one, said that the definition of a psychiatrist is someone who goes to the Folies Bergère and looks at the audience.'

Alex laughed.

'Well, Emily might be just like that.'

When they arrived home Alex put the idea to Emily who was at once thrilled by the possibility, and then Amy, who had come over to see Peter again, asked if she might join them and so a trip for three was arranged to go to Bramall Lane to watch United play Barnsley, a grudge local derby. Alex said it would be unfair of them not to take Chloe and George with them, but he lost that one as soon as he had uttered the words.

The presence of the children meant that Alex too did little in the way of thinking but it was still warm enough for the three of them to be out in the garden with the children in their UV suits even though the sun was not all that strong. It was still relatively safe for the children to be left alone as their moving was limited to crawling but soon it would hard work keeping his eyes on both as they walked and then ran, and probably in opposite directions.

The footballers arrived back shortly before 6 o'clock. Emily was almost ecstatic.
'Two players got sent off and everybody seemed to argue with the ref. The supporters were fascinating to watch.'
'What was the score?'
'Erm, I'm not sure.'
'But did you enjoy it?'
'I've no idea, because most of the time I was watching and listening to the crowd and making mental notes.'
'It's true,' said Amy. 'She really wasn't watching the match, until it turned nasty and two were sent off. She watched that.'
'H'm, well perhaps I'll arrange for Em to go and watch boxing next time.'

After supper Amy (who was intending to stay overnight) decide to complete their afternoon of soccer with a dose of *Strictly Come Dancing*. They could tell from the look on his face that Peter was wanting to watch it too but was torn as Alex and he were going to continue their discussion of the morning.
'Alex!' said his wife loudly, 'mum and I need Peter with us for a little while, so can you wait an hour.'
'I guess I will probably have to. Some things take precedence over all others and on Saturday evenings in the autumn it is definitely *Strictly*.'
This provided Alex with an opportunity to go into the study and do some reading, something which in an ordered fashion, he found difficult to achieve. In this instance it was a book about astrophysics, something about which he knew next to nothing though he had always enjoyed seeing on television those who did know something about it. So much of Christian theology, and for

that matter the various ideologies of other religious traditions, did not take seriously the theories and findings of the very clever men and women who worked in the field of mathematics, physics and astronomy. The sciences had never played much of a part in his education and although he was probably more than competent mathematically, especially insofar as it related to logic, part of the philosophy he had taught at Cambridge, theoretical physics was way beyond him. Perhaps in a way it was also beyond those who engaged with it day by day. How, for example, could any of us get our minds around the thought that everything began 13.8 billion years ago and how on earth did Einstein managed to work out some of the most impossible ideas that have mostly come to pass. Perhaps the only way of dealing with it was to go and join the others and watch the dancing!

Alex and Peter settled down with a glass of whisky each.

'So,' said Alex, 'did any inspiration come during the football match?'

'Yes, two things became quite clear. The first is that I will never go to a football match ever again with Emily. I will say one thing though, she is very canny observer and noticed all sorts of things which I would have missed, though I would have missed them because I was watching the football match I had gone there to see.'

'Yes I sometimes compare her in my mind to the painter LS Lowry because in her poetry she clearly has given expression to what no one else has seen as she has. It's a great gift and sometimes, as you found this afternoon a real pain in the neck and it's why I adore her.'

'I can understand that but what we need to talk about is something that was written on the back of one of the Barnsley defenders. It was his name: Kelly. It took me ages to notice it because they were playing from right to left in the first half and I only saw the names of the defenders when they were playing the other way. And there it was: Kelly.'

'Peter, I am totally foxed, but I trust you, so please tell me more.'

'Assuming Angus was correct that Wilson is the supplier and in the light of your own experience of being unobserved in his office whilst a warder came in and took from his bag the drugs he had brought in, perhaps we can assume that this was a regular occurrence every Tuesday morning. This would suggest he only received them either earlier that morning or on the Monday. I somehow doubt the villains would transfer drugs each Tuesday morning in the same place because it would come to be suspicious and easily noticed, so I think they probably were waiting for him at home on the Monday evening, that someone dropped them off or handed them over to Mrs Wilson. You see, I think Mrs Wilson is involved in this as well. It's more than likely that the governor and his wife are being blackmailed into doing this, and the main reason for blackmail is of course financial. They are being given probably quite a lot of money, money that it has been pointed out to them they need.'

Peter took a drink of his whisky.

'It would help greatly to know what that need is or was but to do that we would need to be able to get access to their bank accounts which is of course totally illegal, but possible. At least it is if you have the right contacts and I have already mentioned her name – Kelly.'

'Peter, if you don't mind me saying so, this is a most odd conversation between a priest in Truro diocese and his former Bishop who ordained him.'

'Yeah, I know. Kelly works for Customs and Excise and is probably just about as clever as you. When I say she works for Customs and Excise what I mean is that she mostly runs Customs and Excise in the south-west. I have now stopped asking her for help with my computer because she does make me feel like a total cretin when she repairs something in less than 10 seconds. Technology of various kinds is her speciality but she's made a special study of the use of technology by criminals. She is based in Bristol and even teaches computer studies on a part-time basis to students at the university, and it is through her that I got the information about the job I'm hoping to apply for. And though you may find this hard to believe knowing me as you think you do but Kelly and I are very much in love.

'She could certainly find out what's going on, where money is being moved and so on. I think villains in the south-west are desperately hoping that she is transferred because she has made something of a total mess up of all their computer pranks. She has a workroom in her basement and it's like entering a spaceship, with screens everywhere constantly working. I'm sure she could make a fortune in the financial world, but what she really likes is walking in the Mendips where we meet quite often and spend most of our day laughing. She is not religious at all and sometimes asks me odd questions such as do I want her to put a block on all religious websites coming into this country from America and I think she means it and I'm severely tempted.

'I'd like to invite her here, to meet the children and you three adults very soon, and I mean very soon. The thing is Alex, not only can she get into their computer brains which is of course a great deal, but she can also get into the way they think and operate, and if need be she could call on help from local colleagues. I totally agree with your Dr Daly that you must not in anyway become involved because Kelly will tell you that it will mean nothing to them to kill you if they think you are doing anything to stop their income.'

'Will she come? This is right out of her area and I imagine she doesn't have much in the way of jurisdiction here. She doesn't know us nor the circumstances we are dealing with.'

'Oh God this is awful. Alex, I have to tell you something that's going to make me feel very uncomfortable. It sounds quite unlikely but there was some smuggling going on in Cornwall, not far from where I live and work. My relationship with the guy I'd been living with had ended somewhat acrimoniously, primarily because I lost all interest in sex which if you're gay and male, is a serious failing. So one day when I probably should have been doing earnest things in the parish, I went for a walk onto the rocks and sat down. I liked it there very much. Whilst there I heard what can only be described as a scuffle or even struggle and when I looked around me I could see a fight taking place between some men who had just got off a boat and others who had obviously been waiting for them. There were more of the latter than the former so the struggle didn't last too long but I was quite taken by the tall leader of the larger group and, in fact couldn't take my eyes off her. She had very short hair and was very slim. I caught her attention and she came over to explain that she was from Customs and Excise et cetera et cetera. We clicked at once a and she said that if I was ever in Bristol she would be very happy to see me. As you know, Alex, it's a long way to Bristol, so it took me all of three days to be there! I was hooked and I still am.'

'I'm not altogether sure what to say. I don't want to congratulate you and make it sound as if I'm relieved you're not gay but I do want to say that you tell a good story, and one that cheers my heart.'

'It doesn't cheer the hearts of some of my gay friends, who think I'm a traitor to the cause.'

'Love is not a cause, Peter, and often, perhaps usually, surprises us in the way it unexpectedly comes. It certainly did for me. I almost said "bugger them" but perhaps in the circumstances I won't!'

They both laughed and Alex topped up their glasses.

'Does this mean you're thinking of making a break with the

Church?'

"We probably haven't enough whisky to deal with that one tonight.'

'And I certainly have no intention of forcing you to do so, but one important thing occurs to me and that it is obvious from where I'm sitting that you caught a chill at the match this afternoon and I think your chances of making Swanwick are not great. I think I'd better leave a message with Colin in the morning.'

'You could be right.'

Chapter Fifteen

Linda was far from happy when Paul told her he would be missing for a couple of Mondays and that someone else would be taking his place "though not in every way", he had said far too merrily for her liking.

'Why?'

'Felicity and me are going on holiday to Tenerife.'

'You've never mentioned her before.'

'No need.'

'And she is?'

'My partner, the person I live with.'

'And does she know about the irregular lifestyle you have?'

'No, but I've sometimes wondered what you'd feel about her coming with me for a threesome.'

'Have you?'

'Yeah. I've been told it's amazing.'

'For the man maybe. So when is it that you're going away?'

'I'll be here next week but it's the following two weeks that I'll be away.'

'And who will be coming instead? Man or woman? If it's the latter then perhaps I ought to get some practice for when you bring Felicity.'

'Hey Linda, don't be heavy about this. As for who will come, that's for others to decide.'

'Paul, can I ask you a question? It's all very well this money coming to us but Karl and Joan and the grandchildren are on their feet again and don't need it anymore. Does that mean Andy can draw a line and stop what he's been doing. After all the longer he goes on the more likely it is that he will be discovered.'

'I'm really pleased for your family that things have now worked out for them and what's been set up here seems to work perfectly. I don't think we'd look too kindly on Andy deciding to stop working for us, and I suspect that if he were to do so it would be much more likely that what he has been doing would become known to the police.'

'Look Paul, you're highly intelligent and able, and as Felicity and I could testify you are also skilful in other ways. Apart from bringing packages to me every Monday, what else do you do?'

'I think, Linda, you will be happier just knowing what happens on a Monday, which reminds me that it is Monday today and, as usual, I have the hots for you, which I think we need to do something about. I will miss you when I'm away but I will return.'

Peter returned to Bristol on the Monday morning having called Kelly in advance but saying nothing because, realistically, he knew it was quite possible that someone might be listening. Kelly made it a rule only to speak in code and on WhatsApp. Meanwhile the children were back at Fiona's, Emily was in her study writing about John Donne and Alex couldn't settle to anything. In addition to his concerns about the group behind the drug smuggling and murder of Angus, he was worried about Peter. They had spoken together most of the afternoon on Sunday as they walked in the Dales, and Peter had given expression to the sort of doubts and question that soon would make it almost impossible for him to continue functioning as a priest in any context, but as it echoed much of Alex's own disquiet he was unable to do more than largely agree with Peter. They shared a profound sense of being lost, that the ways in which their faith had been nourished had been superseded by sentimental rubbish.

Friday afternoon was much too cold to take the children into the garden and once they had woken up from their early afternoon sleep, Alex knew he would have to be entertainer in chief. They had a couple of stories but quickly became bored and then began crawling and showing the first signs of an ability to create havoc that would almost certainly follow within six months. He had received a note from his successor in Truro, Colin Morris, to wish Peter a speedy recovery and for just a moment Alex had not the first idea what he was talking about. Peter had telephoned on Wednesday evening to say that he and Kelly would be with them on Friday afternoon. Chloe and George loved Peter so it might liberate him for a little while if they chose to play with him and if he chose to play with them. He and Emily had engaged in a confused discussion about how many beds she needed to make up, two singles or one double. When they arrived, he would have to engage Peter in a discreet conversation about the matter.

There was also the matter of the invitation from Dr Daly to visit him on the following day. He had no idea why he had been invited but Dr Daly was one of those people you felt you can trust. It wouldn't be a prank for there would be serious intent behind it. Emily thought she wouldn't come but stay behind with the children allowing for a trip into Sheffield to do some shopping with Amy. Alex thought it might be an idea to take Peter and Kelly with him but it would depend on them and the last thing he wanted to do was force any arrangements on them. If they were sensible, they would go for a walk in the Dales. However, he himself would definitely go.

Peter and Kelly arrived just before 4 o'clock and in time for a cup of tea and a piece of cake that Amy had made just that morning. It would be difficult not to be struck by Kelly. She was unusually tall and very slim and she had a boyish haircut. Someone who thought Emily attractive might not find Kelly so, but Alex thought she was indeed quite beautiful in a very different sort of way. What was immediately obvious was her sense of humour and also her obvious closeness to Peter, and it worked the other way round too.

The children were over the moon to see Peter, as he them, but took a little longer with Kelly, probably because she was so enormous in their eyes, but when she got down to their level when they were in their gym, she quickly won their hearts. Alex hated himself for it but he couldn't stop thinking what good parents they would both make. Kelly was so very pleased to meet Emily and said that once she knew she was coming to stay, she had bought her most recent collection of poems.

'Perhaps whilst I'm here, Emily, you might educate me a little in poetic ways. I've been totally scientific in my education up to the present and I almost still am greatly surprised when poems don't rhyme. I'm sorry to be such a philistine but I am very willing to learn.'

'It so happens thatthe Philistines were a very cultured people and not as they are portrayed in the Bible and I would be very happy to do that for you, Kelly. I do wonder though whether you might look at some of my earlier works which are quite different in content and form, and see if they are any less opaque than the most recent lot. I want to tell you though never to take much notice of reviews and criticisms. Sometimes when I read them about my own work, I don't recognise what they are talking about, and that goes as much for when they praise me as when they don't. When poets and writers get together, they all lie to one another and say they don't read the reviews but of course they do but I've now become quite discriminating in those whom

I read. Those on the left detest me because they believe, quite wrongly, that I was once writing for them, and now I've become part of the establishment they're wanting to overthrow. There was a protest during the talk I gave at the Hay Festival and from time to time my fan mail, of which I might add I receive very little and even then is filtered by my publisher, is less than pleasant. But there, playing on the floor with you, and sitting here next to me is all I need. The rest is hot air.'

It was quite right, thought Alex as he listened to Emily speaking, that very often the most important things we say emerge only in the context of the presence of others. He remembered a cup of tea in Winchester with a Bishop and his wife, when the Bishop told Alex about some extremely expensive book he had just bought (and truly it was – £160 no less). The wife looked up with horror and complained that he hadn't told her about it. Wisely, the Bishop replied that was so but that it was easier to communicate that sort of information in the presence of someone else as it would make it harder for her to hit him over the head with a saucepan. Whether she was ameliorated, or did indeed apply a saucepan, he never found out, but he did think it a clever ploy.

Although Peter had tried to explain to Kelly all the circumstances Alex was aware of in terms of the murder of Angus and the almost certainty of drugs being imported into the prison by the governor, Andy Wilson, after supper she asked Alex to go through it again in case Peter had forgotten something.

They were sitting in the study and Emily came in to provide them with coffee after supper.

'I forgot to ask, Peter and Kelly. Is it one bed or two?'

She might have been talking about sugar lumps in the coffee so little fuss did you make of it. The pair looked at each other and smiled.

'It's quite a cold evening,' said Kelly, 'so I think it would be better if it was one.'

Peter blushed slightly and nodded his head. Emily departed with a smile on her face.

Alex told the story again and waited for Kell'y response.

'The issue of drugs in prisons is, as you know completely out of control and on the whole we don't become involved in that', said Kelly. 'Crime committed inside a prison is a matter for the police, and we are much more concerned with those who are supplying those who take it in. In a high security institution the decision has been made to stamp out all importation of drugs. Cannabis to get you through your six months sentence is one thing, it's quite different when it comes to dealing with lifers and those whose mental capacities are already on a knife edge. But now there are gangs who are trying and in some cases succeeding to get past these strictures. We are most interested in them. At the present time I have not alerted the local Customs and Excise guys but if I need to, I will and I have no doubt that they will respond immediately. What we have to do now is out-think them.'

'You seem pretty confident that you can get together a posse at short notice.'

'That,' said Peter proudly, 'is because Kelly has just received notice of a major promotion. She is now Head of Operations (Technical) in Customs and Excise nationally which means oversight of everything that is going on and providing her teams with the sort of technological backup they can use.'

'Well I suppose congratulations are in order, even if I don't exactly know what your new title means.'

'To be perfectly honest Alex, I'm not exactly sure myself but I'm now at a level of such seniority that I can almost certainly decide what it is for myself.'

'Does that mean you will have to leave Bristol?'

'I'm not altogether sure at the moment but if it does Peter and I will relocate accordingly.'

'That sounds good to me.'

Kelly was up long before anyone else, and by the time Alex came down with the children for their breakfast and early morning play, she had clearly been at work for some time making use of Emily's Mac. Alex made her a cup of tea and brought it into the study.

'Emily is a serious published writer. Her publishers ought to be buying her something better than this,' she said as she accepted the cup of tea from Alex.

'It does what I want it to, but really is quite slow and she would be better off using something a little more expensive.'

'Kelly! If you use Apple products, there is nothing "a *little* more expensive".'

'It would be a good investment though, Alex.'

'Has anyone ever told you how much you look like Brigitte Nilsson when she was younger?'

'I'm glad that you added that,' laughed Kelly. 'I'm 6' 1", the same as her, but she's had seven husbands or partners, five children and is seriously wealthy, so we differ slightly."

Alex chortled.

'And what are you doing on the computer now, if it's alright to ask?'

'I'm looking over computer records at Glasgow Airport dealing with imports due to land later this morning.'

I'll leave you then and return to my slave masters who'll be wanting breakfast.'

The whole household plus Amy gathered for drinks at about half past ten, and Chloe and George were clearly loving the presence of so many, all of whom were paying them attention.

'Is there any chance that I can do the shops this afternoon?' said Kelly to Emily and her mum. 'I don't know the shops in Sheffield.'

'That would be great,' said Emily, 'and perhaps we could go to the Apple shop at Meadowhall, and you can help me a buy a new machine having declared the old one even older than my husband.

'Oh no, not that old.'

Everyone laughed including Chloe and George.

'But will you set it up for me and copy everything from the old one?'

'Is the Pope a Catholic?'

'H'm,' said Alex. 'I'm not sure everyone in the Catholic Church would agree.'

'Well, have no fear. Everything on the old machine will be on the new and still on the old.'

'Which way do we go?' asked Peter.

'Across to Chesterfield and then down to Alfreton and then we use the M1 for a short while as we then go into the city. There is a pub he has suggested, the Bell Inn on the delightfully named Angel Row, where he said there's a good selection of beers (not so good for me as I'm driving) and where we can also get some lunch.'

'Does he know I'm coming with you?'

'I felt I had to warn him!'

'Thank you, Alex.'

After a while Alex glanced towards Peter.

'You may recall that I once said it was no concern of mine who anyone shared their bed with.'

'I shall never forget them because I thought they were the single greatest words I had ever heard and when I left your house, I burst into tears.'

'Oh dear, did I have that effect on everyone, do you think?'

'As far as I know, it was only me and the Archbishop of Canterbury and for quite different reasons!'

'Well Peter, I am going to repeat them now because it's still true that it is no concern of mine who anyone shares their bed with.'

'Yeah, but that's not entirely true, is it? I suspect that no less now than then you are concerned for my welfare, whether leaving the ministry or being in love with Kelly. As the great Dennis Potter once wrote, "Am I right or am I right?"'

'He's a great miss. I shall never forget the effect upon me of watching *The Singing Detective*. It was outstanding and then there was *Blade on the Feather*. Genius. However did they get Michael Gambon looking like that with that awful skin condition, though if I'm totally honest the thought of Joanne Whalley ministering to me as she did to him would almost make having it worthwhile.'

'She was also quite brilliant in *Edge of Darkness*.'

'She was. In those days before religion I used to enjoy programmes like that because they really made me think. Having children is utterly wonderful but in the evening if you try to relax watching something on the box, falling asleep is ever so easy, and I very much hope death will be as easy. But returning to the matter in hand, you know how highly I always valued you, Peter, and so it's true that your welfare matters to me a great deal, but it's also true that it's primarily your concern and none of my business.'

'But you're the only person I feel I can say that I would trust my life with. I couldn't ever talk to my parents about my sexuality for example and indeed the only person I ever did do so with was you. My college principal was just too embarrassed ever to mention the word sex. He had children but how I just couldn't imagine.'

'I have to say I don't know very much about how sexuality functions when it's not altogether clear. When Emily and I got together in America it was crystal clear. I do know that some people claim to be bisexual or, as it used to be called, AC/DC.'

'Gosh, I've not heard that phrase for a long time.'

'But is that how it is for you now you're with Kelly?'

'If any of my former gay contacts were to hear me say this, I think they'd be appalled. When I got to theological college I had had very little, if any, sexual experience of any sort. I'm sure you're well aware that some theological colleges, especially in the high church tradition, are like a homosexual convention. When I arrived I found many of the gay students highly amusing and participants in the same sort of religion as me, so I largely went along with the culture which was very camp. I soon became aware that there was more to this and occasionally I used to see sweet-looking young men about the place late at night. In my second term I had a note from the vice-principal to call in on him one evening. I liked him very much and he seemed to me to be an excellent priest. I think that within an hour of arriving at his room, I was in his bed. It was my first sexual experience and being naturally stupid, I assumed that I too must be gay. After all I had chosen the gay boys to be my boys, those I went around with.

'I have to say I wasn't very keen and wondering around town recognised that I looked at women not men, but it has been made clear to me that I was gay, and so I was gay.'

'Had there been any repeat of the incident with the vice-principal?'

'Yes, four more times I think.'

'When your college report came to me, there was no mention of this but if what you said about your principal is true, that's hardly surprising. But what did surprise me was that you came and told me. I was really moved by that and,' he said with a smile on his face, 'it enabled me totally to bugger up the plans of the Archbishop to put together a list of gay clergy to be held at Lambeth.'

'Ooh, I'm rather impressed if I played a part in that.'

'Did you live with anyone in the parish?'

'No one at all. From what I've heard others say, it's not at all easy or even possible in a parish.'

'Yes, I can believe it.'

'I still have gay friends but for some time now I've been convinced that I'm not actually gay. And on my first meeting with Kelly I knew it was so, because from that first moment and in my regular visits to Bristol, she's become everything to me.'

'You have always cheered me up Peter and it's no less the case now. But have you any idea what you want to do now?'

'I haven't asked yet and she might say no, but I want to marry her.'

'That's very old-fashioned of you.'

'I know but despite the extraordinary technological skills she possesses, and one of her colleagues told me one day when we were all having a drink together, that they truly are extraordinary, despite that, in many ways she's very old-fashioned, though I'm pleased to say it does not extend to excluding me from her bed.'

'You are of course thinking of moving to Bristol to be with her and take this job you mentioned but if she has to move, it means you have to move and seek employment wherever she has to go, and of course that may be London. Would you be looking for a parish? The new Bishop of London is a lovely person and I know she would be very helpful if that's what you wanted to do. Anglo-Catholic clergymen on her side are few and far between so she really would welcome you with open arms which would be a pleasure in itself. It's certainly an odd thing, fancying the Bishop of London!'

'I have no ideas to be honest, Alex, and until we know where we're going to be living, I can't even begin to make plans but I honestly couldn't foresee myself being the vicar of a parish, I really couldn't. I didn't know this before I trained because such realities were concealed from us and I have no desire or interest in winning "converts for Jesus" all spending most of my time dealing with finance and meetings. For me, the reality of God is still at the centre of my being but, if you will mind my French, the church always seems to fuck it up. So I think all I can do is give myself totally to Kelly and then adjust.'

'That's more or less exactly what I have done with Emily. Enabling her to create is my greatest gift to her.'

The sat-nav took them exactly where they needed to be, and having parked the car round the back, they made their way via the back door into the pub itself, only to be greeted by a large smile from a man looking not unlike Dr Daly, wearing a grey full length cassock or robe and round his neck chain with a pectoral cross.

'Welcome Bishop Alex, welcome Fr Peter,' said the Orthodox priest.

Chapter Sixteen

As yet, not a word had emerged from Alex's mouth, so stunned was he.

'And you, Alex, what do you want to drink?' asked the priest.

'Er, erm, J2O, any sort.'

Peter looked at him and laughed.

'You look as if you're emerging from an anaesthetic.'

'Well, wouldn't you? He gave me no clue when I saw him.'

'That was surely right and proper. You were consulting a doctor not a priest. He was being properly professional.'

The priest returned with the drinks.

'I think we should probably stick to Tony, Alex and Peter, don't you, even though one or two might address me as Fr Anthony.'

'What sort of Orthodox are you?'

'Very.'

They all laughed.

'As usual with Orthodoxy the answer is complicated. I was an Anglican priest and then received into the Russian Church, in which I was ordained and we founded a Russian Church here. But there has been something of a Russian Revolution and the Patriarchate of Moscow indicated it existed here for Russians only which is perhaps fair. So quite a few of us including our bishop had to find a home elsewhere and now we belong to the Ecumenical Patriarch.'

'Do you still have your own bishop?'

'Sadly no. He incurred the wrath of the Russians in Moscow for changing sides, and became so fed up he asked to be laicised, though 'fed up' may be an understatement on my part. One thing I know about the Orthodox is that they are always falling out with one another, sometimes in a very big way, pronouncing anathemas all over the place. The secret is not to take any notice. There are those of Eastern extraction who maintain Orthodoxy belongs only in the East but the diaspora is now extensive.'

'So you don't miss the C of E then?' said Peter.

'Not in the slightest.'

'But something brought you to Orthodoxy,' said Alex.

'Someone. I attended a conference for those interested in relating medicine to matters of faith. It was mostly awful, but one speaker addressed my heart and at the end I went outside to speak to him before he left, and he invited me to call on him in the following week. I did so and on the following day I resigned my Anglican orders at the diocesan registry, and a week later I was received into the Russian Church at the Cathedral in Ennismore Gardens near Hyde Park.

'The speaker was Metropolitan Anthony, Archbishop of the Moscow Patriarchate and in him I recognised the reality of God. It wasn't learning something from books, it was direct encounter with the being of God, and to this day I continue to know this encounter, not least in the Liturgy, and I will take you to see our Church. It's just down the road.'

'Has it been difficult combining this with your work in Sheffield?' asked Alex.

'Metropolitan Anthony was himself a doctor, so we were able to talk about it freely, but the answer is No.'

Peter and Alex later admitted to one another that their

knowledge of the Orthodox tradition was scant. Alex had known there was an Orthodox community in Cambridge but had had no contact with them so they both listened attentively to all that Tony told them. He spoke mostly of Orthodoxy as a religion of encounter with the divine with a totally different theological tradition to that of the West. He had discovered that he had to unlearn a great deal of Western theological methodology and approach, a religion of ideas and propositions. He had to come to terms with a mystical theology at the centre with the Liturgy holding everything together.

'I suppose the thing about orthodoxy is that it can't be learned from books only experienced and I just about grasp that now.'

'Are there many of you here in Nottingham?'

'Some Orthodox young who are studying at the University come to be with us and they bring a great richness of different traditions, but we have a core of about 50, mostly former Anglicans and one or two former Romans.'

'That's quite a number,' said Alex. 'Are they mostly refugees from the ordination of women?'

'I won't pretend that there weren't some, but I have always made it clear that it was an insufficient reason to want to become Orthodox, because essentially it was a negative reason and if someone chooses to be received, then it has to be because they think this is the right thing to do. In other words they have to choose Orthodoxy rather than reject something else.'

The landlord came to their table carrying two plates of food, one each for Peter and Alex.

'Don't ask me where Fr Anthony's food is because apparently it's the first day of the Advent fast. I hope it doesn't catch on or he'll do me out of business.'

'Is that really so?' said Alex.

'Oh yes. The Orthodox are really keen on fasting and are always doing it. I have begun to get used to it now but at first it was a real pain, but our feast days are quite wonderful and make up for it.'

Alex and Peter finished their lunch, and they then set off down the road towards what looked like the sort of building Methodists or Congregationalists, as they were, would have built. Inside however there was no mistake. The building was full of icons and a sanctuary area cut off by a giant screen and curtains. Peter noticed that there was nowhere to sit.

'If you're old or infirm,' said Tony, 'then you can sit at the side, but in Orthodoxy everyone stands. Former Anglicans can find this very difficult at first because our services are very much longer than they would have been used to. Our normal Sunday Liturgy for example, lasts about two hours and that's a long time to stand if you're not used to doing it. Greek men in particular, tend not to come into the service until it is at least halfway through and nobody thinks that less than normal. People move around, kissing icons and one another, and many don't receive communion all that often, mainly I think, because they're meant to go to confession before doing so.'

Peter's phone rang.

'Excuse me, I'll take it outside.'

He hadn't been gone long before he returned looking anxious.

'Alex we've got to go now. Emily has been assaulted and although she's okay and Amy has the children, she wants you with her.'

'Don't delay,' said Tony. 'Go straight up the motorway, it's Saturday so she'll be in the Hallamshire. I'll be in touch.'

Peter and Alex ran up the road to the car park behind the pub and were quickly on their way.

'I assume that was Kelly on the phone.'

'It was.'

Alex drove up the M1 faster than he would normally do. It wasn't all that far, but he was desperate to get there. Once they arrived at the hospital, Peter told Alex to get out and into A&E and leave the parking of the car to him. Alex went straight into the Department and up to the reception desk and said who he was.

'I'm told your wife will have something of a shiner over the next few days, but the police told me that the big girl with her was phenomenal, knocking out with a punch one of those who had attacked your wife and making sure the other one didn't leave the scene.'

Anxious or not, Alex could not resist a smile.

'She is waiting for you and I'll call the staff nurse and ask her to bring them both through.'

As Emily fell into his arms, he could see what the receptionist meant by a shiner. They walked through the waiting area and out of the door before speaking.

'Before you start saying I have been heroic,' said Emily, 'there was only one hero, and that was Kelly.'

'It was nothing and trust me, I've known worse.'

Reaching the car, Alex put Emily into the back and joined her there, so that Kelly could sit alongside Peter in the front.

'We had already been to Meadowhall and bought a wonderful new Mac, and then came back into the city centre. I'm pleased to say that when it happened, Amy was well ahead with the buggy and so the children didn't see what took place. There was a stall with lots of material about Momentum and other left-wing causes and we had just passed it. All of a sudden two of the young men behind the stall were standing in front of me. The first one said, "Well, look who it is, the traitorous Miss Cunningham, the lackey of the Tories". I took no notice and continued walking and that was when the other person punched me. Perhaps he hadn't seen Kelly with me, well he would be advised to go to the opticians, because a second or two later he was out for the count on the ground, and the wonderful Kelly had apprehended the other in such a way as to ensure he was going nowhere. Someone must have called the police because they were there in seconds. I won't pretend it didn't hurt and heaven knows what the twins are going to think when they see me, but really I'm fine.'

'What happened to the two youths?'

'I've no idea. Do you know, Kelly?'

'No. By the time we were on our way to the hospital the police had taken them away but where to, I have no idea, though I'll find out when I've got the new computer up and running.'

'Do you mean you can break into the police computer in Sheffield?' asked Alex.

'Good heavens, no,' she replied with a broad grin. 'I have open access to them at any time because of my work.

'And presumably that means you can discover the state of play with regard to investigations into the murder of Angus Smallwood.'

'I've already done that, and as you suspected it's not receiving a great deal of attention. As yet though, no one has made any sort of link with drugs which probably means that we, meaning you Alex, Peter and I are going to have to do a little investigation of our own. I'm sorry Emily but you can't be involved. There are the children to be cared for and then at the moment you look like a criminal, though that gives me an idea. Let me go and unbox, as they say. It won't take me very long and I'll make sure everything on the old machine is transferred to the new because I brought with me a snazzy little gizmo that can do it very quickly and safely.'

'But what about me?' said Amy. 'Surely there's a part for a sweet old lady in your plans?'

'Perhaps there is, Amy,' said Alex hurriedly, 'but we don't know any sweet old ladies!'

'My dear son-in-law, I would check closely in your sausages for broken glass if I were you!.'

Emily was made to lie down on the bed, Amy was in the kitchen, Kelly in the study whilst Alex and Peter fed the children and then took them up for their bath which they greatly enjoyed. As they were putting on the pyjamas, Peter said to Alex, 'We haven't had much chance to talk about Nottingham given all that's happened since. What did you make of it?'

'As with what happened later, it was a real shock, discovering Dr Daly had an entirely different persona, to say the least, and I was really sorry we had to leave when we did because there were so many more questions I wanted to ask him. I can't deny that I was moved by the experience. The things he said made a lot of sense to me. Faith as encounter rather than an accumulation of bits and pieces of knowledge is what drew me in the first place and for which I was always searching thereafter and never found. I certainly don't and can't make any kind of sense of the Western God imposed upon us by virtue essentially of geography. I've reached the stage when the God of Catholicism and Protestantism for me has died, or at least I would like to hope so.

'Tony made abundantly clear that temperamentally, coming in the main from where they do in Eastern Europe, the Orthodox have an astonishing capacity to hate one another, but so do liberals and evangelicals in the Church of England, so when he also spoke of direct encounter with God I warmed to what he was saying, but he was talking about a religion in diaspora, which is always of a certain character, most notably romantic. Most of his people are English and perhaps visit Greece or Istanbul or Russia for their holidays but in terms of realism, they are not Greek or Russian, and that leaves me feeling somewhat uneasy about it.'

Looking at their daddy and thinking he was telling them a story, Chloe and George seemed fascinated by his every word, but then again, so was Peter, who now offered to read them a real story from a book, and a book with pictures – in other words, a real book!

Once in their cots, Emily came in and kissed them both. George in particular was interested in the colour of her eye and reached out to touch it. Typically, however, Chloe did not notice it because Chloe was already asleep. Emily left them and joined Alex and Peter downstairs and just a few minutes later, Kelly emerged from the study and reported that she had finished and asking what she should do with the boxes. Alex said he would attend to them after supper, the aroma of which already had them salivating. When all was ready, Alex was pleased to discover that all his sausages were pristine.

'You haven't told us about your trip to Nottingham though I thought I overheard someone say that you had a shock to discover your psychiatrist was in fact an Orthodox priest,' said Amy.

'What?' said Emily and Kelly almost in unison.

'Unlikely though it is, he is, and when we met him in the pub, we met him in his grey cassock with a pectoral cross, everyone calling him Father Anthony. He bought us a sort of Nottinghamshire Ploughman's lunch but ate nothing himself because it's the first day of what he called the Advent fast, which is something apparently they take very seriously. As neither of us knew a great deal about Orthodoxy, to our eternal shame, he provided us with just the right sort of introduction, and then led us down the road to his church, which thirty years or so ago they bought from the Methodists, I think he said.'

'Yes, it was from the Methodists,' added Peter.

'I haven't heard yet what Peter thought about it, and of course it was not in use when we were there, but I was spellbound by it. It was exquisitely beautiful with amazing icons everywhere and nowhere to sit. No chairs, no pews, as everyone remains standing throughout the Liturgy, though there were a few seats at the side for those not able to manage two hours or so.'

'I agree totally with Alex. Father Anthony spoke about the necessity of encounter with God, rather than learning things as happens in the scholastic philosophy and theology of the West, and when I went into the church, I could see what he meant. It was quite amazing.'

'Was Fr Anthony in recruiting mode?' asked Amy.

'Well if he was it was very subtle, and I'm sure I heard him say that they don't ever proselytise and feel that they don't need to do so. It was very impressive and I shall certainly at some stage make the effort to go and experience the Liturgy with the community, but what I really liked, what really tickled me, was him saying that nobody cared when you arrived for the service. You might come at the beginning or halfway through, but no one was interested in that. It's not like that in most Church of England churches I can tell you,' said Alex.

'I would like to know a little more about this, but can I briefly change the subject?' said Kelly. 'I will need to do a little more work this evening, but I'm very much hoping that by tomorrow we shall be in a position to draw up a plan of action. I know full well it's the week of the Parole Board, and it's important that nothing interrupts that, but I would very much like us to go into action on Monday morning and there is a certain urgency about it because one of the principals acts on Monday morning and is then intending to go abroad for a holiday, so I think we will need to strike while the iron is hot and before he goes and gets even hotter in the sun. Are you happy for me to lead a briefing in the morning with you all, though I'm sorry Emily but I just can't find a role for Chloe and George though there might yet be one for you.'

Everyone looked round and nodded their approval, though having heard of her pugilistic skills in the centre of Sheffield that afternoon, they were hardly likely to do otherwise!'

In bed Emily lay in Alex's arms feeling safe and secure.

'Do you think, darling, that the time has come when perhaps I should lay aside writing poetry? Today's experience and what happened at Hay has really set me wondering.'

'It's quite ironic. Oliver wanted me to accompany you to the US to protect you and stop boys and girls who wanted a piece of the action from someone they adored, mauling and groping you. Now it's the opposite. The people who abused you this afternoon were motivated by a silly ideology that doesn't know how to cope with those who think differently from them. You know as well as I do, and everyone who reads you, that you are a poet through and through and you could no more stop being that than try to give up breathing for a day. But if you want reassurance, just give Nicky a ring and tell her what you've just said to me.'

'Oh God, I wouldn't dare.'

'Yes it's hard to know who to be most scared of – Nicky or Kelly?'

'Don't be silly darling. Kelly can knock you out with a single punch. Nicky can do it with just a look!'

Chapter Seventeen

After a late Sunday breakfast for all but Chloe and George, who had decided that they wanted very early breakfast, much to their daddy's discomfort, and who were now out on a cold November morning with Emily in the hope that they might get to sleep, the others gathered together in the sitting room.

'I do like that new machine that Emily bought yesterday. Just perfect,' said Kelly.

'Our bank balance wasn't quite so impressed by it,' added Alex with a broad smile.

'So what I need to do is to tell you where I have arrived at and then suggest a way forward. You will of course understand that now being in charge of Customs and Excise operations I usually work with crack teams who take everything in first time and always get it right, and that is certainly the case with every operation I have undertaken apart from all of them. So don't be anxious if it doesn't go in immediately.

'Ostensibly I'm concerned with the question of drugs being brought into the prison but because I'm sure it's drug-related, the murder of Angus Smallwood is also at the fore of my mind. I'm delighted to discover that I'm up against someone who is also pretty good with computers and IT. That makes it something of a challenge. Perhaps he has a degree in the subject but, like all of us, he is prone to mistakes so sometimes he is not as secure as those he works for assume he is, probably because he thinks he's safe and can't be bothered to to go the extra mile, and if he worked for me he would be out of a job straight away. I have been looking closely for those occasions. I know who he is. That bit was easy because those who make contact with him usually do so without any precautions at all. His name is Norman Bartholomew, the same surname of Eric Morecambe. He has a live-in girlfriend called Felicity who rings her parents at least three times a week, though I suspect Norman knows nothing of that, and she is an excellent source of intelligence because she tells them everything. His work name is Paul and every Monday morning he pays a visit to the home of the governor of the prison, Mr Wilson. It's almost certain that is how the consignment reaches Wilson, who on Tuesday morning takes it with him into work. From hints, sometimes far from subtle, Paul stays quite a long time with Mrs Wilson, and she has taken something of a shine to him. Why is it people need to boast about having a lover? Well, she does, to her friend Kate, and doesn't spare her blushes. Paul also brings with him, as well as what he might be making use of between his legs, large amounts of money, usually £2,000 a week though early on there was a £5,000 payment. This money was used to support the Wilson son, his business, his home, his wife and children, who were in serious financial difficulties which have now disappeared as a result of regular injections of cash deposits. I imagine that it was the son, unknowingly, that provided the reason for the blackmail necessary to persuade Wilson to do this, though it has alerted me to others across the country who are in a network and pass on information about who might desperately need money, and so be open to similar forms of blackmail, which I have passed on the police already.

'I don't think Paul personally would have had any part in the killing of Angus Smallwood but I suspect he made the arrangements, and it wouldn't surprise me if he was given a handsome bung for doing so, some of which he might well have passed on to the young lad who did the killing, who probably needed it to keep up his own supply of drugs. Eventually we shall have to leave that to the police in Hull. They've done sod all so far but they will – I'll make sure of that.

Wilson is small fry and Mrs Wilson gets her reward every Monday. I do want Norman but I'm more interested in those who are pulling the strings, who are providing and presumably making a lot of money.'

'Kelly? How do you know the content of phone calls that took place in the past?' asked Alex, 'and don't you require a warrant or a licence of some sort to tap telephones?'

'Alex, when you were a bishop in the Church of England did you ever have to deal with disciplinary matters with regard to the clergy?'

'I was only there two years, remember, but yes there were one or two matters like that, and by the way not with Peter.'

'I'm glad to hear it but would you here and now provide us with the details?'

Alex smiled.

'I take your point and I should never have asked.'

'I'm only teasing you, Alex. As Director of Operations I'm now able to issue licences.'

'Do you know where Norman lives?' asked Peter.

'Yes. What I don't know is whether he receives the consignment on Sunday evening or collects it on a Monday morning before he visits Mrs Wilson.'

'How will you find that out?' asked Peter.

'I have some help arriving later today, two of my Bristol team that Peter knows and has even danced with.'

'Don't tell me: Crystin and Jenni?'

'Yes.'

'And tomorrow?' asked Amy.

'Tomorrow morning we shall observe Paul paying his visit. After he leaves I shall pay a visit to what is I imagine the post-coital Linda and have a conversation with her. At the moment she is planning to go and stay with her son Karl and his wife Joan for a brief holiday – presumably while Paul is sunning himself with Felicity. I will endeavour to persuade her that she should go a day early and let her husband know. If she plays ball we will forget her completely because though she is complicit in the conspiracy, nothing would be gained by anyone to have her in court. This, I think convince her to do what I ask and Crystin and Jenni will give her safe passage on to her train in York. If she fails to cooperate, I will have to lean on her a little to the extent of saying that her husband will learn about her Monday mornings with Paul, and that I will insist on waiting with her for the arrival of the drug squad, and inform her of the sort of typical prison sentence she can expect, whilst her husband will deny all knowledge of the presence of drugs in the house.'

'Please don't ever lean on me, Kelly,' said Amy, and they all laughed.

'I understand, Alex, that the Parole Board will take place on Tuesday morning. Is Wilson due to take part?'

'He has made a written contribution but won't attend the Board which is made up entirely of independent members.'

'Ok. Let's leave it there for now. Can the girls call in for a cup of tea this afternoon, Amy?'

'Of course. The more the merrier.'

Coming in from the cold with the children Emily's eye looked a distinctly awful yellow, but she was smiling and the twins were asleep, and learning that two others would be joining them later, was delighted, not least because she could see how much Amy was enjoying herself. Mother Superior was trying into Guest Mistress! The main meal would be this evening but Amy had been prepared for lunch with lots of cartons of Covent Garden soup and baguettes and cheese. Alex endeavoured to bring Em up to speed on the morning's briefing and she was relieved to know that Alex would not be on the 'front line' of any activity.

Teddy Armstrong was enjoying his last Sunday morning in prison, so confident was he that he would be given parole on Tuesday even if it took a few days for it to be enacted. His confidence was built above all on his knowledge of the governor's Tuesday morning activity, and although he had told him that once he was out, he wouldn't think of it again, perhaps he had been a little economical with the actualité. He never knew when such information might come in useful. He also knew, though so did most in the nick, the identity of the screw who distributed the stuff. Mr Pickles might well be spending more time in prison than he had assumed, once Teddy got to the police. The man was a top-class shit anyway and would deserve all he got.

Sunday afternoon meant a visit to the KCOM Stadium to see Andy's beloved 'Tigers': Hull City FC, today against Bristol City. With his mate, Al, they had good seats near the Director's Box, where they could see the owner Assem Allam. Andy originally came from just across the Suspension Bridge, a place called Barton-on-Humber, so his appointment to Banklyn could not have been better. It turned out to be a good game with the right result: 2:0 to Hull. Andy and Al were delighted, and there was more delight to come as his wife Linda-the-never-satisfied (as thought of her), was going away on Tuesday to stay with Karl and Joan, leaving him the house to himself and whomsoever he might invite in. Linda showed no interest in sex any more.

Crystin and Jenni were already clued up when they arrived. They were both Welsh. Each lived with their boyfriend in Bristol but often worked together and the level of trust between them was considerable. In her absence they said that Kelly was an outstanding boss but did point that there were urgent changes she would need to make in terms of Peter's dancing! They had a cup of tea and some cake before going into the study for a private briefing with Kelly. They then left in their somewhat updated version of a Camper Van.

'Will they be sleeping in that tonight, Kelly? It's not warm out there,' said Emily.

'Don't worry, they're Welsh!'

The two women parked at least 150 yards away from Norman's house and were facing away from it, each in turn sitting in the rear and keeping a close watch, noting every vehicle and pedestrian that came and went in the street.

'Poor Emily,' said Crystin. 'That must have hurt.'

'Not as much as the punch handed out by Kelly, I bet.'

'Did she say anything about any sort of follow-up?'

'She read the police report which said one of them was being charged with assault and both with affray.'

'That's good.'

'He's a nice man, the former bishop I mean. Apparently their love story is quite wonderful, and her black-eye notwithstanding I've got to admit Emily is stunningly attractive. The bishop must wonder if he'll wake up and it's all a dream.'

Their inane conversation continued for ages, but they were great friends at work and outside, so were perfectly happy together. Shortly before nine o'clock however a car come towards them and then turned into Norman's drive. Crystin took as many photographs as she could using a military camera fitted with night vision, whilst Jenni left the vehicle and walked to the end of the street and back, pausing only for a moment in which to attach a small device under the car.

'Well, Felicity, are you looking forward to your holiday? Norman has been working hard, so he deserves some time off. Where is he by the way?'

'He had a curry last night which didn't agree with him, but it would be nice to think this is his last visit of the day to the loo, and yes we're both excited by the hols.'

'You are flying Thursday?'

'Yes, from Robin Hood.'

'Well here's a little extra for you both,' the man said, handing her an envelope, 'but don't spend it on curries!'

'Thank you. That's so very kind of you.'

'Not at all, he deserves it.'

Norman entered the room looking somewhat the worse for wear.

'Vindaloo?'

'Jalfrezi – never again.'

'Famous last words, but will you be ok for work tomorrow? I can always get someone to cover for you.'

'I'm sure I'll be fine.'

'The case is in your hall as usual and I may need you to cross the Pennines on Wednesday. It won't take long once you're there, but the gentleman I need you to see has been badly bereaved and I want him to have something that might help, but we'll speak later about that. So I will return home. My wife thinks I might have a fancy woman whom I see every Sunday night though I've said that if I have I'm the fastest worker in the country.'

The three of them laughed and the man and Norman stood.

'Once again, have a good holiday, Felicity, and you, Norman, take better care of yourself than you managed last night.'

'I'll try my best.'

Crystin and Jenni watched the man leave and drive his car away which immediately showed on their screen, waiting another ten minutes before setting off in their van in the opposite direction. They drove to a camping site which as this time of the year was more or less deserted other than the hardy regulars who lived there all the year apart from the statutory six weeks they had to spend abroad for tax reasons. Crystin began to prepare their evening meal while Jenni transferred the photographs to the computer and forwarded them to Kelly. In the meantime the car they were tracking was heading into Beverley.

Kelly was frustrated by the quality of the photographs and made mental note that better night sights were essential, but one or two showed his face a little more clearly than the others and would have to do. She sent them off straightaway for recognition, though it was not until shortly before four o'clock that a message came through, which she received when she got up at five. There was an 80% recognition which, given the dark, was pretty good. She sent this through to Crystin and Jenni, who were already on their way to Long Riston and the house of the Wilsons, where they were expecting to see Norman arrive before too long.

In Pooley Bridge and Penrith Tom and his former wife, Mattie, were preparing themselves to be collected by a paid-for taxi to take them over to Yorkshire. Neither had slept well and didn't expect to do so at the Holiday Inn where they due to stay tonight so that would be ready first thing for the Board. They had both decided that they would make their statements in the absence of Armstrong. They wanted proper and lasting justice for their daughters and Tom knew that he would get it one day, somehow.

Reggie Dickinson played golf on most Monday mornings which gave him a chance to catch up with his friends. Reggie had put a lot of money into the Club and was highly regarded by members who not only knew he had money but also knew he played off a handicap of just two, which was pretty impressive for an amateur, and the word was that he would be Club Captain next year. This morning he was looking forward to the 18 holes before him and failed to notice a very tall young woman taking photographs of him with a large telephoto lens, photographs which once again were being transmitted for recognition and which produced the result of 99% certainty that these were of Reginald Dickinson, who had, earlier in life, done time for robbery with violence. He also had on his record a non-custodial sentence for running a brothel. At the present time there was nothing he could be charged with but Kelly never objected to waiting.

The lovebirds of Long Riston were meeting one another's needs.
'I wouldn't fancy it myself at this time on a Monday morning,' said Jenni.
'Nor me, but he's a fit looking lad, and a lady of her age might be glad of whatever and whenever she can get it.'
Crystin's phone rang.
'On my way,' said the voice, and was gone.
The two women looked at one another and laughed.
'Great conversationalist, our boss,' said Jenni.
Ten minutes later they saw Kelly arrive and park her car. Nothing now happened for some time. Clearly one or other was storing up nuts for their time apart. Eventually Norman emerged and drove away. Kelly waited ten minutes before leaving her car and walked up the drive towards the house and rang the doorbell. By now she had turned on her microphone and everything could be heard and was being recorded.
A rather flustered lady in her early fifties answered the door, her hair all over the place.

'Mrs Wilson? '

'Yes.'

'My name is Kelly Ramsey and I work for Customs and Excise, and I have here a warrant to enter your house.' She handed over the document. 'I also have two colleagues nearby who can hear all our conversation and can join me if need be. Please may I come in?'

Linda opened the door wide enough for Kelly to enter and she showed her to a seat in the sitting room.

'You'll miss Paul.'

Linda looked shocked.

'Mrs Wilson, how you spend your Monday mornings is not something I am remotely interested in and have no wish to disclose to anyone, nor am I judging you in any way. I saw him leave and I could see the attraction.'

Despite herself Linda smiled and blushed slightly.

'Please may I call you Linda, and please call me Kelly'

'Of course.'

'Let me say at once that I am not especially interested in involving you in any way though I'm sure you know what I am interested in, which is to say the contents of the container in the hall which I noticed as we came in. When others, such as the drug squad, become involved, it would be best for you to be a long way away, as I know you are intending, when you go to stay with Karl, Joan and your two grandchildren.'

Linda's eyes opened in amazement.

'Do you know everything about me?'

'Of course not, and in any case, as I said earlier, I very much hope you can be left out of this completely. Paul brings a parcel for you every week and do you or your husband transfer it to his briefcase?'

'He is insistent on doing it himself so he can check what's inside in case there's a dispute about it.'

'Well I can understand that. Some of those who are running him would take exception to something going missing.'

'I can assure you he doesn't use any of it himself.'

Kelly smiled.

'Yes, I have no difficulty in believing that. Do you know what the package contains?'

'Illegal drugs – that's all I know, and it's all I wanted to know.'

'Yet you agreed to your husband doing this to save your son's business and their house. '

'Wouldn't you?'

'Linda! How old do you think I am?

They both laughed.

'As I'm sure you are aware, your husband is guilty of a very serious crime and will almost certainly be going to prison for a very long time, but he is actually nothing more than what we call a mule – someone who simply carries the merchandise and hands it over to another. The police will no doubt attend to him, but we are looking for his controllers, those who have blackmailed and manipulated him into doing this for them. Have you any possible idea how this might happen? I can't think they would speak to him at his workplace but what about here? Does he receive long phone calls?'

'Not that I can recall but I do know he stops at a particular pub on his way home most evenings for a pint, to unwind, he says. It's called the Bluebell in Old Ellerby. He's never mentioned it but maybe that's where whoever he sees, meets with him.'

'I really don't think it would be very fair of us to expect you to relate to your husband this evening keeping the knowledge of my visit to yourself so I am going to insist that you go to visit your family today instead of tomorrow. If there was a small crisis, say a sick grandchild, and you had decided you needed to go and help, how would you inform your husband?'

'He doesn't welcome me telephoning him at work so what I

would do would be to text him, but if he knew one of the children was ill, he would be on the phone to them straight away and discover that it wasn't so. I think the best thing for me to do would be to say that I can't see any point in hanging about until tomorrow when I'm ready to go and I would say that the postman has been, which he will understand.'

'How long will it take to get ready Linda?'

'I will need a shower!'

Kelly nodded her head.

'Yes, that might be best.'

'But I'm mostly packed so not too long.'

'I thought you might have more objections.'

'If it hadn't been for the mess Karl was in I would never have agreed to any of this in the first place but Andy said it was completely safe – the stupid bugger. Will anything come out about Paul and me?'

'If it does, it doesn't represent anything that you've done which is criminal. Right, I'd like you to go and get yourself ready. When you come down my place will have been taken by Crystin. When you've completed your packing, she will ask you to send a text message to your husband. Don't respond to any reply he sends but go with Chrystin and her colleague Jenni (and I ought to warn you that they are both Welsh, but it can't be helped) who will take you to the railway station in York and see you on to the train safely.'

'Welsh, did you say? Two of them? That's not fair!'

'I know but life's tough. I have to work with them all the time!'

They grinned at one another, and then Linda went upstairs.

'Actually, I love you, Welsh girls!' said Kelly.

Chapter Eighteen

With Amy back home in Sheffield, Peter and Kelly doing something somewhere, and Chloe and George with Fiona, Alex and Emily were luxuriating in silence, until that is, the telephone rang and someone asked to speak to Emily. It was the editor, no less, of *The Star*, the Sheffield daily paper, checking up on the rumour that Emily had been physically assaulted in the city centre over the weekend. Happily, Emily trusted this particular editor a great deal, and they got on well together, and realised that she would not sensationalise anything that had happened.

'To be honest, Nancy, the shock that it happened at all was far worse than the pain of his punch, but I had a friend with me who was able to take care of him and make sure he didn't repeat it. My two children are very impressed by the colour of my eye, but I'm perfectly okay. I have had some hassle from left wing youths before now so I'm beginning to get used to it, but it's an unhappy state of affairs.'

Mention of the two children distracted Nancy from the question of the black eye and they were able to talk 'little people' for the rest of the time.

'I like her but can't think what she's doing as the editor of a newspaper. Surely she should be more interested in salacious gossip and things that aren't true!' said Alex.

'I know,' replied his wife, cuddling up to him, 'what's the world coming to? Time was when you could rely on the news media to report the deaths of those who were still alive.'

'I'm glad we weren't killed though. Just imagine never knowing Chloe and George.'

They kissed.

'I'd like to hear about your visit to Nottingham which I so rudely interrupted.'

'Yes, I'm sorry. There hasn't been much time to be able to tell you, and in any case I have needed to give it some thought. First, I was completely taken aback by discovering Dr Daly was also Fr Anthony and in the circumstances who wouldn't be? Although I had no sense that he was offering me the reality of Orthodoxy, as something I should be considering, nevertheless I got the impression he was fashioning what he said with me in mind. I didn't mind that, and he really is a very nice man. He didn't attempt to speak theology, possibly because he mistakenly thinks I know more about it than him which is most certainly not true, but he spoke of faith as the encounter with God, almost face-to-face, and there's no doubt I warmed to that. I'm pretty certain he was relying on an article in the Observer which appeared when I became a bishop, in which I talked about my initial experience in the small church in Cambridge near Peterhouse. He rightly discerned that if anything was going to have an impact on me it was in that sort of language – where we encounter God directly almost regardless of the churches. He then took us down to see his church, and I suspect that although he has made it over legally to the community, he paid for a great deal of it himself. Orthodox churches are very beautiful and a strange mixture of simplicity and complexity which is compelling. At one level the many icons are simply paintings or copies of paintings, albeit made in a special way, and you can see them at that level, but they are also windows into heaven and you are present there with the Saints depicted before you. There is also that wonderful smell of incense which means it doesn't have that characteristic odour so familiar in churches of the Church of England, mostly consisting of polish. And then, Peter received his telephone call, and we had to leave.'

'To hear you talking about it my love, I find quite moving, because in the time that we have been together, I've not heard you say anything even remotely like it, except on the day Anne-Marie got married in that wonderful church in Edinburgh – Old St Paul's I think it was. You almost sound as if you believe it, I'm not objecting to that if it is so, because more than anything else in this world I long for your happiness and fulfilment, and I would even sacrifice any further writings of my own, for you to achieve that.'

'That is such a wonderful loving thing to say though there is no way you could stop being a poet, and not just any poet but the best. I'm so glad you don't do social media which must be a great cause of frustration to some people, positively and negatively, but I do think you should regard the hostility you sometimes engender as proof positive that you are doing the right thing. I'm so pleased Kelly was with you but I'm sorry I wasn't there to help defend you.'

'I do hope something genuine and long-term develops for Kelly and Peter.'

'I agree. They are such lovely people. She will need considerable patience and love for him because there's a lot of adjustment he needs to make and that will take time. He is quite an emotional person, and he is always susceptible to bearing the imprint of the last person who sat on him, if you take my meaning. I almost think he's waiting for me to tell him what to do.'

'But what are *you* going to do? That is the most important of questions? Would you be interested in pursuing Orthodoxy?'

'Leaving on one side, though only for the moment, the nationalistic intercine warfare that goes on between the various groups in Eastern Europe and elsewhere, and although I do find what Father Anthony said quite attractive in terms that it links in with my own earlier experience, it's difficult for me not to see it as just a sort of exotic hobby, something esoteric and attractive but actually not related in any sort of way to daily reality. Once I'd figured out how to use the new computer, I had a brief look this morning at some of the Anglicanised Orthodox groups in this country, and so very often I was just struck by how incongruous they are, with their priests wearing stove-pipe hats, trying to give the impression that they were Greek, when actually most were Anglican priests at one time or another, most of whom converted when women were ordained.

'Most telling of all were some comments on the Russian Orthodox Church website, explaining why it had been necessary to make substantial changes after the death of their former Archbishop, and it was precisely because it had all become Anglican-Orthodox and a rather prissy drawing room spirituality, all a little upper-class, which I think on the whole you couldn't say that about how it is lived in Russia, Greece or the Ukraine. I wish them well of course, but they don't take even slightly seriously the critical thinking characteristic of the West and which they mostly deride. If I was to go over, I wouldn't last long.'

Emily looked at her watch.

'We must be setting off for Fiona's soon. It's been your Parole Board this morning, hasn't it.'

'Gosh, I'd almost forgotten. I wonder when they'll let me know their decision.'

'What's your bet?'

'No idea. I hope he stays where he is but you never know. He's a sly person and really quite unpleasant.'

Teddy had woken early, if that is, he had slept at all. It was the big day, the day he had been preparing for some time, for which he had adopted the role of perfect prisoner, reformed prisoner and suitably penitent prisoner. It was also Tuesday morning, when the governor would be bringing into the place things he should not, information which he intended to use when appropriate. He knew it was unrealistic for him to expect to be out of here today but with a positive result it would take very little time. At breakfast even some of the most foul of people wished him well, no doubt hoping that their own time would come soon. They had seen how he did it and others were already striving to do likewise. When news of his release was made public, he would be some sort of hero.

He had been a little disappointed that the victim statements would be made in his absence as he had already worked out for himself a script of total remorse but hoped it might still be used in the course of the Board. He would not learn the identity of the three people who would determine his fate until they arrived, which was frustrating, to say the least as it meant he couldn't look them up on the internet. Now all he had to do was to sit and wait for the arrival of his legal representative and receive any wisdom she might have to offer, though he got the impression that the solicitor chosen for him was probably the most junior they could find.

Tom Kiernan and Mattie Gathercole were collected from the hotel at 8.30 and delivered at the Prison twenty minutes later. Both were extremely nervous and just wanted it over with. Once they passed through security, they were led to a room, formerly that of Angus Smallwood, in which to wait. They had decided between them that Tom would go first.

'This is the nearest I've been to Armstrong since he was

sentenced. If only I knew where to find him there would no need of a Parole Board.'

'That wouldn't help the girls though, would it?'

'He's a smarmy git, and he'll try everything he knows to convince them he should be released.'

'If they do, will they let him come back to the Lakes?'

'Oh no. They'll give him a new identity, move him somewhere else and probably help him to get a job. That's not what I call justice for our daughters. He's had 20 years, and they have had life, and for that matter so have we.'

The door opened and in came a smartly dressed man who introduced himself as the prison governor who went over the process awaiting them, though they knew this in papers from the Ministry of Justice.

'The Board members are almost ready to begin and will introduce themselves to you. The other person present is Armstrong's legal representative who may ask you to clarify anything she doesn't understand but can't cross-examine you as in a court of law, and if she tries she will be stopped from doing so. As you both requested, Armstrong will not be in the room, and will not be brought from his cell until you have left the building. The car to take you home will be immediately available to you outside with the driver ready and waiting. Have you any questions?'

They both shook their heads.

'I am charged with looking after a lot of people here who have done terrible things, and although I do it every day of course, I try my hardest never to forget their victims. In doing this work, it's you above all that I have at the forefront of my mind, and that is certainly how it is today.'

Tom and Mattie again nodded their heads.

'Who is coming first?'

'Me,' said Tom.

'I'll have someone bring you a cup of tea, Mrs Gathercole, though I don't imagine we'll be all that long.'

Andy led Tom out of the office along a corridor and into a room used normally for educational purposes, where, before him sat two men and two women, one of the women looking as if she was there doing work experience from school.

When both had made their statements they were at once led out of the prison by Myles, the deputy governor who saw them into their car and away. Only now were they able to speak.

'Well?' asked Mattie.

'It was all very low key. They listened in silence and when I'd done, they thanked me and I left. His lawyer said nothing.'

'She did me. Asked to clarify my present position and congratulated me on making a new life. Only the woman in charge spoke otherwise, like you, to thank me and wish me a safe journey back to Penrith.'

'Well, we've done our best and now all we can do is hope that the bastard is turned down or falls down the stairs and breaks his fucking neck.'

Like a well-rehearsed actor Teddy came on stage confident that his performance would have the effect he desired. The three making up the decision makers pushed him hard as he knew they would, and he listened carefully to what they said to see if he could detect whose written report they were relying at various times in their questioning. At the end he still felt confident enough not to succumb to the temptation to grovel. His brief said nothing and was a total waste of space, but he knew that the verdict of the Board would be brought to him by her though she would not be present as the decision was made. The chair suggested they waited until after lunch before giving consideration to the matter in hand, which irked Armstrong when his brief called to see him. It was a burst of anger that ran counter to the self he had spent the morning wanting them to believe in and greatly surprised her.

It was at about three o'clock when the chair informed Armstrong's solicitor that they had made their decision that her client was to be given Parole under license, allotted an alias and housed in Leeds. He would not be allowed within 50 miles of Pooley Bridge or Penrith nor make any kind of contact with person or persons within that 50 miles. He must meet with a Probation Services Officer every week without fail. He would also have to observe a curfew. Any breach of these conditions would result in his immediate re-arrest and return to prison to complete the rest of his sentence for which a further application for parole would not be accepted. His release could, at the convenience of the governor, take place at any time from midnight onwards providing their decision was ratified by the Secretary of State later that afternoon. The young solicitor left the room and was conducted upstairs to Armstrong's cell greeting him with a broad smile, though not as broad as his.

The Panel first informed the Justice Ministry and spoke to a minion who informed them that the Secretary of State would confirm all the decisions taken around the country at 5-00pm. They then asked to see the governor, who simply followed the protocol and thanked them for their work. He said he would see the prisoner and make arrangements for his release. What he didn't mention to them was his relief to be getting rid of the wretched man. There was a lot of paperwork to be completed and Andy arranged for tea to be brought in for them all.

'Was it straightforward or am I not supposed to ask?' asked Andy.

'The Board's discussions are completely confidential,' replied the Chair.

'Of course, forgive me.'

'Have you others coming up, Governor?' said the first man.

'No. It's rather different here from, say, a local prison when it's a regular occurrence.'

'What do you think of the addition to the team of the Liaison Officer?' asked the second man.

'I think it's a really good idea, and it's my belief that we have been served in this regarded by Dr Elliot.'

'The one submission we lacked was from the prison chaplain, but I gather you've had a terrible tragedy in that regard.'

'Yes, it's the supreme irony, working here with some of the most dangerous men in the country, that he was stabbed and robbed on a night out in Hull.'

'Has anyone been arrested?'

'Not yet, but I gather the police are working flat out on it.'

The Chair stood.

'That's everything done. The Secretary of State will complete the process at about five o'clock and you should receive a telephone shortly after that from the department authorising the release, though I'm sure you're familiar with the process.'

'I am.'

'Thank you for your hospitality throughout the day. You will find that I have left an emergency number on your desk should any questions arise. Someone is there 24 hours a day.'

They shook hands and Andy himself led them downstairs and out to the main gate. On his way back he bumped into Officer Pickles.

'Everything ok this morning?' asked Andy.

'Got it all done by the time the Board arrived.'

'Good man. Well we're getting rid of the piece of shit you'll be pleased to know.'

'I am.'

Perhaps you could go and bring him to my office and I think it would be a good idea if you stay.'

'Of course, governor.'

Andy decided that this was turning out to be a good day and to celebrate he would go to an exotic little club he knew. Linda was away so why not? The Beatles were quite wrong then they sang "Money can't buy you love." The sort he wanted it could!

He decided to keep Armstrong standing, just to remind him where he was.

'The normal time for departure is 7.00 am with someone to collect you but I very much doubt that anyone will. You will be given a bus and train warrant to take you to Leeds and you will make your own way to the hostel in Oakwood. You must be there by 11.00 or you will be in breach of your parole license and find yourself in Armley Jail. These warnings are absolutely serious. Once there, you will informed as to other regulations. I know you were hoping for Derby but there we are. Your solicitor will have informed you of the other terms of your licence.'

'Yes, she did.'

'Well, good luck.'

He stood and shook his hand.

'And good luck to you both,' he gestured towards Pickles, 'Must be a good little earner. Everyone here knows that Wilfred here is involved, but it's just the three of us who know how it gets in.'

'I think we agreed that once I got you out of here, you would no longer remember it.'

'Absolutely Andy, and so I will. It's like car insurance, you forget about it completely until you need it. You just never know, do you?'

Teddy was returned to his cell with a smile on his face, and when he and Pickles had left the room, Andy picked up his phone, dialled an outside line and spoke a few words.

Norman and Felicity were beginning to pack, getting excited about their holiday when his mobile rang.

'Ok, just let me get some paper to write the info down. I can go first thing. Won't take long, and is that all? Ok.'

'Who was that, Norm?'

'Just my boss. He has a courier job for me tomorrow. I'll leave early and be back by dinner time. Fancy coming. Across the Pennines, nice scenery?'

'On the day before our holiday? You are kidding.'

'Just a thought.'

Kelly and Peter arrived back to find Amy babysitting, with Alex and Emily at the cinema in Buxton.

'Where have you been?'

'York,' said Kelly. Lovely city and horrendous traffic. 'It was a test to see if Peter could manage putting up with me in clothes shopping mode.'

'And?'

'It rather backfired as it became more a matter of seeing if I could manage putting up with him in clothes shopping mode!'

Amy laughed.

'But it's been great having some time off together.'

'And what about the Welsh wizards?'

'Alas, no time off for them though they'll make up for it.'

'They did spend some time in a pub this evening,' said Peter.

'True, and the last I heard they were on their way into Hull.'

Andy had taken Linda's car, which he thought quite wise. It had been a good day and he intended having a good night. He had been reassured earlier that everything would be taken care of with regard to Armstrong and was sure it would be, so in terms of finance he was set up for a long time to come. He continued to do his job well and although the Inspection was on the horizon, he had no real anxieties. He'd even managed to ditch the wretched Smallwood. In such a happy frame of mind he didn't notice that he was being followed.

'The Place' was exclusive and only for those with a lot of money, and catered for those who wanted just a little more for their money than was available elsewhere. The scrutineering prior to membership was rigorous and more than a few of the Hull great and good were members, including a number of women, which Andy always thought bizarre. Some members travelled from long distances to have their tastes catered for, there being nowhere quite like it for many miles around.

Crystin and Jenni followed him to the car park and then shadowed him up to the door of the club. They had no desire to enter but wondered whether Linda knew what her husband was up to whilst she was away though it perhaps accounted for lack of sadness that he might be going to prison. Besides which, she didn't need to watch others cavorting on a stage, or whatever they got up to, given her own private source of entertainment every Monday morning.

Their instructions from Kelly were to spend the night observing anything that Norman might be doing, so they set off, fortified by fish and chips, and eventually stopped a hundred years or so from where they could see his car.

Chapter Nineteen

Crystin and Jenni were tired and still asleep and so missed Norman leaving shortly after 5 o'clock. They had no tracker on him so there was little they could do but eat some breakfast and report back to Kelly in Derbyshire, who was sitting with Amy looking at the children who were crawling every which way.

'How is it going, Kelly?' asked Amy.

'Too fast, I'm afraid, and I may have to find a way to slow it down.'

'Can you do that?'

'I think I'll have to have a go, but I'll wait for Crystin and Jenni to get here and we'll talk it over.'

'Please tell me if I'm overstepping the mark, but do you give time to thinking through not just your work issues which must be considerable, but also your relationship with Peter. I don't think either of us have known him very long and although I think he's an absolutely smashing bloke, up with the best, do you think he may still be confused or uncertain about his sexuality? I only ask because I don't want either of you to get hurt and it may be that it's only someone of my age who can ask the question.'

'Thank you for mentioning it, Amy. I'm sure others have thought it but only you have had the sense to ask it. Without being unnecessarily prurient I can tell you, though I wouldn't tell anyone else, that he doesn't just perform satisfactorily in bed but wonderfully well. I think that's a positive sign, as far as it goes. I know full well and so does everyone else that I'm what some would call boyish – tall, short hair, not curvy, and perhaps he feels happiest with that but I don't think he's had all that much gay sexual experience and he says that he found it not really to his liking. Somehow or other he got into a gay set and just assumed that is what he was.'

'I first met him in Windermere as we were coming out of a shop. The former Bishop of Truro, my son-in-law, spent most of the rest of the day waxing lyrical about him and saying he was probably the finest priest he had ordained or was in the diocese. Alex is no fool and a pretty shrewd judge of character and now I've had a little more contact with him, I too am impressed. A bit like Alex he has yet to find his path in life but I feel quite strongly that if the pair of you can continue to make a go of it, I would feel pretty hopeful for him, and for you.'

The children now had to be rescued from where they should not be and each adult brought one back.

'I have noticed that you're both very good indeed with Chloe and George so you may need to think that one through. It's so much easier for women to return to their work in terms of continuing to do what they did before, which in your case is considerable, but the real difficulty is an underlying exhaustion that almost all mothers feel.'

'Do you know Amy, I could use someone like you, someone to talk sense into our young people.'

Amy laughed.

'Don't go saying that in the presence of Emily. She is quite likely to say "What, that interfering old bat".

A voice came from the kitchen.

'Which interfering old bat are you talking about?' said Emily.

'Your lovely mother.'

'I thought so. The title sounded about right, but the important thing is that she knows we all love her.'

Myles had come in to make the final arrangements with Teddy for his release, making sure he had the various documents he needed, and going through with him again the instructions he had to follow as he made his way by bus to York and then by train to Leeds. Again he was told that any breach of the probate conditions would result in an immediate return to prison. Myles went with him to the gates which were opening electronically.

'Well good luck Armstrong, you've been a model prisoner, now go and be a model citizen.'

They shook hands though Teddy did not reply and he walked out, a free man, across the road and waited for the bus. Looking back, the gates had already been closed and he had succeeded in getting free, he had conned the lot of them, made total mugs of them, but he did not come away empty-handed. How he could use the information about the governor's smuggling drugs into the place, at this stage he didn't know. But he did know that he would use it and wholly to his own benefit. The bus appeared and in no time at all Teddy was well away from prison and had no intention of ever returning. He had wanted Derby but Leeds would have to do.

Norman parked the car well away from the house. He stopped at the gate and looked around but things were pretty quiet, the children presumably having gone to school. He opened the gate and walked up to the front door. There was no bell, so he knocked and waited. Eventually Tom came and opened the door peering out.

'Mr Kiernan?' asked Norman.

'My name is Harry Robertson and I work in the prison service, and it struck me that you might well want to know the result of the parole board you took part in yesterday. I don't think it will help either of us to know how I have obtained the information which you will eventually receive in writing from the Ministry of Justice, but I can assure you it's accurate.'

Tom pulled the door back and ushered Norman in.

'Well?'

'I'm sorry to be the bearer of bad news but Armstrong has been given parole and indeed will have left prison two hours ago.'

'My two daughters were not released from their hell two hours ago and now he can do whatever he pleases.'

'From later this morning I gather he will be living in Leeds, in a halfway house, a hostel for newly released prisoners and he will be bound by very strict regulations, and he will only need to break one and he will be back inside.'

'I expect he's got a new name, something like Mr Totalshit would be most appropriate.'

'No, he's Mr Ronald Scott – he didn't get the choice, and he is living at 15 Turner Street in the Oakwood area of the city which is a lot better than he deserves.'

'Well I'm very grateful to you, very grateful indeed, so thank you for coming. I knew the bastard would get out. He is a liar and a cheat and a murderer, but he's not going to get away with it for ever.'

Norman took his leave, hoping that he had done enough, and after stopping at a cafe for a bacon butty was once more on way home and then on to the sun tomorrow.

The ladies from Wales had arrived and breakfasted with Amy. Emily was intending to write all morning and Alex and Peter had taken Chloe and George to Fiona's. Alex could not help but notice and be greatly encouraged by Peter's reaction to Fiona. She was an extremely attractive young woman and knew how to dress to bring out the best and Peter responded accordingly, not the response of a gay man he presumed. On the way back Peter was able to talk a little about his own reaction to Nottingham.

'I've always thought of myself as Anglo-Catholic. It works for me or at least it worked for me in the past. The nineteenth-century guys are my heroes – Keble, Williams, Dr Pusey and many others. Entering that Orthodox Church with Fr Anthony was quite a shock. I didn't have the near mystical experience that you had. I just stood there and wondered what any of it had to do with the price of fish, and when the phone call about Emily came, I felt that even more. It was an exotic but wholly incongruous place, and I suddenly realised that the kind of religion I was used to and thought I was coming to continue providing for people was like that too. I know we spoke very little as we flew up the M1, but I was having to cope with thoughts I found and find profoundly disturbing.'

'Interestingly I said almost exactly the same to Emily yesterday morning. I don't know if my psychiatrist was trying to encourage me to join them, but everything within me rebels against anything sectarian, and in my short time in Truro I was alarmed at the signs that it was happening rapidly within the Church of England, and in no small measure that is why I got out and will be staying out, which reminds me, yesterday I received through the post an official document signed and sealed by his grace Gordon, Archbishop of Canterbury, officially taking away any residual spiritualities I might possess. I certainly don't know what he has to do with the price of fish!'

Kelly and her colleagues sat in the kitchen with cups of coffee on the table.

'I think we are approaching the end,' said Kelly. 'That will inevitably mean bringing in the police and I would love to know if any or how many senior officers were present in The Place last night when Wilson went in. All the evidence suggests that they have been less than assiduous in seeking to find the murderer of Angus Smallwood, and I'm left wondering whether certain officers were complicit in it. Norman and Felicity are supposed to be going on holiday tomorrow, and as yet they don't know it, but they're not. His travel company, aka me, are sending him communication today postponing their departure until Saturday morning, which will give us just a little more time to act without alerting the two we are really after: Wilson and Reggie Dickinson.'

'Though they'll only be the end links in a long chain,' said Crystin.

'Yes, but maybe not. I've been doing a search of known associates of Dickinson and it just might be that he's a link higher up the chain than we might have imagined. I have a trace that puts him close to the Pope.'

'How close?' asked Jenni.

'He was in Pentonville with the Pope's son, Joe, and he is up to his eyes in merchandising. We've been trying to tie him to imports from Germany but so far he's used a string of intermediaries and doesn't touch the stuff himself.'

'So how do we or the police get Dickinson?' asked Crystin.

'For drugs probably not, but we might with the help of our friend Norman, who with his partner Felicity is having a bad day, get him for conspiracy to commit murder.'

'But that's not our business, boss,' said Jenni.

'I totally agree but if we can provide the information that will kick the Humberside Police into action, they just might get there, which I very much doubt otherwise,'

'So what's the plan?'

Norman and Felicity were fed up. It was only a two-day delay, but it felt like it was two hundred. Norman had received both a telephone call and an email from the holiday company, and simply as a matter of course traced them back to see if they were bona fide, which they were. The company was offering considerable compensation which helped ameliorate their feelings a little. Norman knew that overbooking was a deliberate policy on the part of airlines because they could normally rely on enough people not turning up. Felicity rang up one of her friends who lived at Hornsea and decided she would go over to spend the afternoon with her and her children. Norman said he would stay at home as there were a couple of programmes he had recorded but not yet seen and there was no shortage of beer in the fridge.

Kelly had listened into Felicity's call and her trip to Hornsea was perfect as far as Kelly was concerned as it meant they would have access to Norman alone. The three of them had an early lunch and set off just as Chloe and George were arriving home with Alex. He hadn't quite got used to being an outpost of Customs and Excise though he was by no means unhappy with the female company.

They stopped, as before, 150 yards away from Norman's home. Felicity's car was still in place so all they could do was wait, but once she had gone, Kelly and Jenni would swing into action, leaving Crystin to monitor and record everything from the vehicle. They had not been there long when a police car pulled up behind them, from which a male and a female officer came up to the van and knocked on the window which Kelly opened.

'A resident has drawn our attention to your repeated presence here. Would you mind telling me what you are doing and can you please show me some identification?'

'First question – no, because it has nothing to do with you. With regard to your second question, I'm the head of Customs and Excise and at the moment you are buggering up an operation just by being here. This is my identification and don't take it amiss, but please piss off.'

'Shouldn't we have been informed?'

'I said piss off, and do it now.'

The two officers returned to their car, reversed into a driveway and disappeared.

'There will be a complaint you know,' said Jenni.

'I expect so, but as the complaint will end up on my desk, I couldn't give a toss. The only thing that matters is that we haven't spooked Norman and Felicity.'

Tom found the hostel easily enough even though he had never been to Leeds before. When he asked for directions from various people they were always helpful, even though some of them were darkies, of which there were clearly a large number in Leeds, totally unlike Pooley Bridge and the Lake District as a whole though not unlike prison of course. As yet he hadn't worked out the manner in which he would confront Armstrong or Scott as he was now known, so he walked down the road and had something to eat and drink in a café he had noticed whilst parking his car. He still went over in his mind the question of the identity of the man who had brought him the information about Armstrong on the previous morning, and continued to think that it could only be someone who hated the man as much as he did and resented the fact that he had been released on parole, which Tom still regarded as an abomination. Whoever he was he was grateful to him even though Armstrong would not necessarily share his gratitude.

More or less on time, Felicity reversed out of the drive and headed off for her afternoon in Hornsea. Kelly decided she would wait at least 15 minutes to give time for Felicity to return having forgotten something. She received a phone call.

'Hello. Oh hi Helen, how are things? Well your timing is perfect – do tell. Really? That's most odd but there's someone I can speak to about it. Yes okay and thank you.'

'Important?' asked Jenni

'I really don't know but it was information that our friend Norman tripped a number of cameras on his way to and back from the Lake District yesterday. I wonder what he was doing there.'

'I wasn't aware you had his car under surveillance,' said Jenni.

'Well what its significance is I have no idea. We'll wait another five minutes and then go and pay Norman a visit.'

Tom was not expecting to be returning home and the burger and chips he was eating was his equivalent of the Last Supper, a thought which amused him greatly. His waiter looked as if he was a Paki, but seemed nice enough for all that and throughout his meal he kept his eyes peeled for any sign of Armstrong.

Inside the hostel Armstrong was feeling strangely uncomfortable. Over the years he had heard stories of how difficult it was settling once you were outside. At the moment he stuck to his room much as he always had to his cell and was uneasy at the thought of going through the front door, and certainly going into the city centre. But he had been away for a very long time and the outside world had changed considerably. Even on the bus and train on the previous day people of all ages seem to be engrossed in their telephones. The man in charge of probation in the city had said he would come to see him sometime this afternoon to discuss the possibility of employment. At the moment he had no bank account, and he suspected that to purchase one of the ubiquitous telephones would cost considerably more than the money he had been given when he had left prison the previous morning, but in any case he wouldn't know who to call. It wasn't quite what he had expected it to be once he had achieved parole. Could it be that he was missing prison?

Tom finished his lunch off with apple pie and custard and a mug of tea. As he left the café, the waiter wished him a nice day and insisted he come again. Well, he was intent on the former, but there was no chance of the latter. Walking up towards the hostel he felt buoyed up. This was the moment he had been longing for. He stopped in front of the door and fiddled in his right-hand pocket, which to a casual observer might have suggested someone searching for a key. He rang the doorbell. There was no answer, so he rang it again. This time the door was opened by someone who looked to Tom like a sort of Eastern European tramp.

'I'm sorry,' he said, 'but we are having dinner.' His accent was thick and certainly East European. 'Have you come to see someone in particular?'

'Well I would hardly be knocking on this particular door if I hadn't,' said Tom. 'I've brought some important papers from the parole service for Mr Scott.'

'I can take them for him.'

'I don't think so. They are legal papers and have to be handed over only to Mr Scott, and you are wasting my time, so please go and ask him to come. It will only take a few moments.'

The man turned his back on Tom but left the door open, and then, suddenly, for the first time in 20 years since he was sentenced, coming towards him was Teddy Armstrong. He would have recognised him anywhere but Teddy seemed oblivious to who the man at the door was.

'What do you want?' Teddy said.

'I'm sorry to interrupt your lunch Mr Scott but I needed to see you as I have something for you.'

Tom pulled his right hand out of his pocket and with it a revolver which he had bought some years ago in the hope that this day would come.

'Well Teddy,' he said, 'you should have stayed in prison. It wasn't just my lovely daughters you murdered, but you murdered me as well. As I am already dead, I have long since vowed that you must go the same way.'

There was a loud bang and Teddy hit the floor clutching his groin. Tom wasted no further time and now put a bullet into Teddy's head. By this time people from inside the house were coming towards him, so he did what he knew he had to do, which was to put the barrel of the gun into his own mouth, and pull the trigger.

Chapter Twenty

Norman had just fetched his first bottle of beer from the fridge and was settling down to watch some episodes of Eastenders that he had missed. Though he had been feeling pretty cross when the air company rang, at least he knew it was only a delay and that they would be going on Saturday. Much to his frustration, the front doorbell rang, He paused the television and went to the front door where, much to his surprise, there were two rather dishy young ladies standing in front of him, one of them being quite tall.

'I take it you're not Jehovah's Witnesses,' said Norman, 'though if they're all as pretty as you two I might just join.'

'I'm Kelly Hanrahan and this is my colleague Jennifer Arnold, and we are from HM Customs and Excise, and I have here a warrant to enter your house, where I hope we can have a conversation.'

'Course you can though you're quite lucky to find me in. We were meant to be going on our holidays this morning and our flight was postponed until Saturday. Anyway, come in.'

The two women were experienced enough to recognise that Norman was suddenly ill at ease and trying very hard to make it look as if he wasn't. They sat down.

'So what can I do for you?'

'Whereabouts did you do your degree in Computing and IT?'

'The University of Northumbria.'

'Was it a good course?'

'I learned a great deal and I'm still able to put some of that into practice day by day.'

'Yes, I know but I have to say, having observed some of your work, that the one word that springs to my mind is 'careless'. You will know as well as I do that most people are in using their computers and telephones, mainly because they think it won't happen to them or that what they are communicating isn't all that important, and sometimes they are just being bone idle. I wonder which it is with you.'

'I not at all sure where this is leading.'

'Well, in the first place let's deal with Monday morning and your regular tryst, shall we call it, with Linda Wilson. I suspect that Felicity knows nothing about this. Am I right?'

'Pointless question.'

'I'll take that as a no. So what happens between you and Linda upstairs is known only to the two of you?'

'Yes, that's always been part of the deal.'

'The thing is, Norman, or perhaps in this context I should call you Paul, Linda has spoken about this regularly to her closest friend and, I might add, in some considerable detail, but I will spare your blushes. Actually Norman, what you get up to upstairs in the Wilson house is of no interest to me at all. What I'm interested in is what happens downstairs, when you arrive, and what you bring with you and leave with her. That is much more important to me. But what is even more important to me is a man called Reginald who delivers it to your house every Sunday evening, and for which I am sure you are paid handsomely.

'We know where and how the package you deliver is taken elsewhere and distributed. The police are especially interested in that and I think they already have all they need in the way of evidence. But it will come back to you, as the mule bringing it from your house to that of Andy Wilson. They will therefore be coming for you and I wouldn't build your hopes up too high about getting away on holiday on Saturday.'

'All I do is take it and leave it in Long Riston, and believe me I have no knowledge of what is inside the package other than knowing it is probably illegal substances. I get paid for that not as much as you might think though I also get Mrs Wilson thrown in as an extra, but in all this my part is minuscule.'

Kelly's phone rang.

'Yes Crystin.' She listened intently, looking at Norman throughout.

'When? Ok. Yes, tell them we'll still be here. Bye.'

'Your car was clocked a number of times on the M6 north and south yesterday morning. Would you please tell me what you were doing and where you were going?

'It had nothing to do with Customs and Excise. I was carrying nothing illegal. I just was taking some information to someone.'

'Tom Kiernon?'

Norman shrugged but said nothing.

'I had an opportunity yesterday to look closely at your non-WhatsApp calls list. I'm interested in one number, but I shall hand it over to the police forensic team though as you and I both know they will need to be told what do.'

Jenni stood and went to the window.

'They're here,' she said.

'You'll be leaving here for some considerable time, Norman, and not flying anywhere on Saturday. Your cancellation today was due to me by the way. They'll never know but you were sensible to check up even though you only got me.'

Jenni had opened the front door and allowed the three officers in, having first informed them who she and Kelly were.

'Good afternoon. I'm Inspector Bob Moorman, this is Sergeant

John Wood, and this is Constable Alan Heath, and we're from Humberside CID.'

'You're very welcome Inspector,' said Kelly, 'and we should be very happy to leave you in a few moments but I wonder whether you and I might catch a word together outside first.'

He was more than happy to go along with this and together they left the house and walked a little down the drive.

'I think we probably owe you a great deal.'

'The person to whom you owe most is the Reverend Angus Smallwood. It was he who alerted us to what was going on in Banklyn, and for which he paid a heavy price. I'm absolutely certain that Norman here was asked to arrange that murder, to ensure the Banklyn scam continued because it was clearly a good earner. Then we have what happened in Leeds earlier today. The man murdered was released from Banklyn yesterday, and yesterday morning Norman was instructed to drive to Pooley Bridge to inform Tom Kiernan of the release of Theodore Armstrong and give him the needful as to his location. Tom's two very young daughters were abducted, raped and murdered by Armstrong and I think Tom's only reason for living was the hope that he might avenge what was done. Then his life's work was complete.

'Drugs of various kinds were being transported on a Sunday evening from Beverley to this house, and on a Monday morning to the home of the prison governor, Andy Wilson. Every Tuesday morning he took them into Banklyn in the certain knowledge that he and his deputy were not searched nor sniffed by a spaniel. A witness says he saw a prison officer enter the governor's office in his absence, remove what was inside the briefcase and presumably then distributed it all among those prisoners whose families outside were paying the bill.'

'Blimey, you have been busy. This witness, is he reliable?'

'It all depends on whether you regard a retired bishop of the

Church of England as reliable. He was in there doing work for the Parole Board, but knowing him as I do I think you can take his reliability for granted.'

'This murder of Angus Smallwood we put down to being a hate crime and the motive robbery, but you think it was more than that?'

'I know it was. You will have to find him but I do at least know the number of his mobile though it took me quite a while to find it. If you will allow me to handle Norman's phone for just a minute or two, I should be able to tell you his name.'

'I'd heard a rumour that you are a clever bugger, but I didn't realise that you were that clever!'

'I'll take that as a compliment. There is one other thing. Do you know who I mean by the Pope?'

'Don't we all?'

'His son did time with someone called Reginald Dickinson, who lives in Beverley. This is the man who brings the merchandise each Sunday evening to Norman, and seems to be running this particular operation. I'm not going to tell you how to do your job but I would suggest you pick up Wilson and Dickinson at the same time so neither alerts the other.'

'That makes total sense.'

'Just before we go in there is one other matter. Neither Mrs Wilson who is currently away with her son and daughter-in-law, nor Felicity, the partner of Norman, know anything about any of this.'

'Thanks for that. Now let's go and have a look at that phone.'

Norman was not at all pleased that Kelly should have access to his phone and insisted that he should have access to a solicitor, but as he had not yet been cautioned he was told he couldn't have one. Kelly made things worse for him by asking that the other officers and Jenni should go looking for any other phones there might be on the property.

'I did tell you about being careless, Norman,' said Kelly. 'You see, it's here among your received calls, hidden away but of course accessible. I'd already seen the number. Tolly: is that a name that means anything to you, Bob?'

He smiled and gently nodded his head.

'How did you do that?' asked Norman, genuinely impressed.

'Probably by being on a better course than yours,' she answered with a grin.

Norman shook his head.

'That was clever.'

'Norman you know as well as me that when when you know how it's done it's not actually as clever as it looks.'

'Hey, don't give the game away!'

'Linda will miss Paul.'

'Don't ever tell Felicity, but Paul will miss Linda too.'

'Who are Paul and Linda?' asked Tom, a little bewildered.'

'Just some mutual friends,' replied Kelly.

The search completed and no other phones found, Kelly decided it was time to go.

Reginald and Andy were both picked up simultaneously, one from his home in Beverley, the other from Banklyn with as little fuss as possible. Seeing it happen Mr Pickles went into the staff mess and taking out his phone rang the number he had been given for emergencies. Reginald moved quickly and was already in the drive opening his car door when he discovered that his exit was blocked by two police cars. All in all, Humberside CID had had one of their better days, and the Chief Constable would be delighted and unwilling to recognise any part played by HM Customs and Excise. Even better news followed when he received a report that a young black man had been arrested and charged with the murder of Angus Smallwood. He decided to arrange for a press conference on the following morning.

'I suppose that we could call all that we've done satisfactory,' said Christyn. 'But I bet you we get no credit for it.'

'I know what he did and what he brought about through his intermediaries, which was two murders and a suicide, but I feel really sad about Norman. Linda must have thought she was in heaven every Monday morning – what an amazing looking lad. I almost asked for an hour of extra interrogation with Norman upstairs in the bedroom, but all things considered, probably best not.'

Her two colleagues laughed.

'I know what you mean though,' said Jenni, 'and it's awful to think of him going completely to waste inside and one wonders how the hell he got caught up in it in the first place.'

'Well my sisters, forgive my anti-feminism, but I think the answer may lie in the word Felicity,' said Kelly. 'Did you see the car she went off in, and the furniture in there was not bought at MFI. I couldn't see her properly from where we were parked but the photographs of her in the sitting room were pretty impressive. That's not any kind of excuse to present to the judge but there may be something in it all the same – she wanted money.'

'Kelly?' asked Crystin. 'In the midst of all this busyness, I don't suppose you've had chance to give any thought to where you have decided to be based in your new job, which is another way of asking whether you have decided that in your new base there is going to be someone called Peter living with you and will there be space for a contingent of the Welsh?'

'Yes, I have decided both but I'm not going to tell you just yet.'

'You do know that you're an awkward and extremely difficult boss to work for, don't you?'

'Of course. But you've known that a long time. By the way I expect Alex and Emily will be more than happy to put you up for the night though you may prefer to return to Bristol and your lovely men, but if you can complete the report on what we've done on your machines at home, then I think there's no need for you to come back in at least until a week on Monday.'

'You do know that you are a fantastic and splendid boss to work for, don't you?

'Darling, what's the matter?' asked Emily. She had seen him on the telephone a couple of minutes earlier, but now he looked quite distraught.

'Something quite terrible has happened. First of all I just been told that Theodore Armstrong was actually given parole two days ago, and that he was sent from Banklyn to an ex-prisoners hostel in Leeds. And then at lunchtime today someone called to see him claiming to be from the probation service but it wasn't, it was Tom Kiernan from Pooley Bridge, the father of the two little girls Armstrong killed. Apparently when Armstrong opened the door to him, Tom produced a gun and shot Armstrong twice, once in the groin and once in the head. Tom then put the gun into his mouth and pulled the trigger. It's just so awful.'

'Who was that on the phone?'

'It was Kelly, on her way back here now that they've finished everything in Hull and asking if it will be okay if all three of them stay the night as they're pretty exhausted and don't fancy driving all the way back to Bristol this evening. I said that would be fine – I hope that's okay.'

'Of course it will and in fact I've still got the same bedding on their beds, as I assumed it would be a possibility.'

'There are a number of aspects of this I just don't understand. In the first place, how did Armstrong get his parole? But having got it how on earth did Tom know about it, and even more how could he possibly know where he was living? He was given a new identity and nobody but the probation Service were allowed to know where he was, with the exception of just one person, Andy Wilson, the governor, and the only reason he might be willing to do that was in case his drug scam was known to Armstrong. And how was he in possession of a gun? I wouldn't know how to get one.'

'Phew, that's a relief. Alex, where are the children?'

'Peter wanted to take them out in their buggy as it was such a nice autumn afternoon. I imagine he'll be back at any moment.'

'Don't get me wrong, because I'm extremely fond of him and if he wants to stay he can, but is Peter a permanent fixture?'

'No. He will need to get back to his parish and once he and Kelly have begun to work something out for themselves, he can then resign and take on something new wherever it is Kelly decides to live.'

'So you're convinced it's permanent.'

'Yes I am. When I've been out with him I notice that he looks at girls and women and not at men. You don't need me to tell you that Peter's an attractive proposition, and I feel that is why the gay community tried to convince him that he is gay. They liked to have him with them, but he has come to a realisation of what was going on and he has no blame to pour on others, and I've tried to help him understand that we make mistakes in this life, we get things wrong, and that I am the best example of that to him.'

'And in terms of mistakes we make, have you thought more about your visit to Nottingham and the site of the Orthodox Church there?

'They would only want me to be a priest and to be absolutely frank, I hate beards. It was kind of him to invite me but it's not any kind of possible home in which I could live.'

Twenty minites later Emily heard the front door open and moments later into the sitting room came Chloe and George smiling broadly, followed by Peter with an even broader smile.

'The van has just arrived,' he said, 'and with it three exhausted looking women, whereas these two are wide-awake and full of the joys of autumn.'

The three women trudged their way into the house.

'You think there's any chance of a shower, Emily.'

'You really don't have to ask you know. Of course there is and from the looks of you a shower ought to be followed by a cup of tea and a chance to do nothing at all, even sleep if you need to. My mum is coming over to cook us a meal, Peter is occupied with the children and I suspect you've been doing a very important job, and doing it well.'

'You two bring your stuff in from the van and get yourselves cleaned up,' said Kelly. 'I need to have a chat with Alex if he's around.'

'He will be any moment now. His mother-in-law has sent him out to get something from the shop and as the nearest shop is quite some distance away, he has to take the car, but I love the way he's totally obedient to my mother.'

They laughed. Crystin and Jenni went outside to bring in their bags, though Jenni remained outside in order to let the man in her life know that not only would she be back before lunch tomorrow but that she had the whole of next week off as well, whilst Crystin did the same upstairs before heading directly to the shower.

'So has it been successful?' asked Amy.

'Let's put it this way, there is simply no chance that Humberside CID would have got there without us, and of course they will take all the credit. The two deaths today in Leeds, which I presume Alex told you about, could not have been prevented but at least we were able to provide them with the person responsible for bringing them about, albeit indirectly. It's quite possible, no, it's certain, that Humberside CID will ask

Alex to go to Banklyn to facilitate an identification, but apart from that he and we are done.'

'So will you be heading off back to Bristol tomorrow?'

'Well I haven't had the chance to talk with Peter yet but I'm hoping to persuade him to allow us to keep you from your poetry in the morning, so that we can discuss things, important things, with you.'

'Me? Surely Alex is the one you need to talk to.'

'We've both spoken with him separately and he is a great source of wisdom, but I think that you are the person we need to speak with. If that is, you will.'

Alex returned from his shopping trip at much the same time as Amy arrived. No sooner had he arrived than the phone rang, which Amy answered and then handed over to her son-in-law.

'Dr Elliot. This is Inspector Bob Moorman from Humberside CID. I don't know whether the world's greatest technical wizard has yet got round to telling you but we've had quite a day with various arrests and charges, including one for murder. The Chief Constable will take the glory but it's your friend Kelly who deserves the plaudits.'

'That doesn't surprise me in the slightest.'

'The thing is Dr Elliot, there is one other person to whom we need to speak to help us with our enquiries and as far as we can tell you are the only person who knows who it is as I gather you witnessed this prison officer handling drugs in the Office of the Governor.'

'Yes I did.'

'I know it's a nuisance but is there any possibility that you could meet me at Banklyn in the morning, say 9.30? You have right of access through being the official Liason Officer, and the deputy governor who we have ruled out of any involvement in what has been happening will meet us.'

'That will be perfectly fine. I'll be there.'

Chapter Twenty One

For just about the first time Chloe and George rewarded their parents by both sleeping right through. Normally at least one or both spent the second part of the night with mummy and daddy, which made their decision to buy a super-king-size bed a wise one. When Alex tried to sneak out of bed, Chloe noticed and wanted out with him. Once downstairs he made her a drink and then tea for himself. She wanted to play, though first a nappy change was required by which time Amy had joined them.

'What time do you need to leave?'

'7.30 more or less. Em's taking the children to Fiona's and then Peter and Kelly want to talk something over with her.'

'Could you cope with a passenger, Alex?

'It would be great. Thank you.'

By the time Alex and Amy set off, only Emily and the children were up, feasting on breakfast cereal. Jenni and Crystin had said goodbye and thank you on the previous evening. They had before them an unpleasant journey around Birmingham and on to the M5.

Neither Alex nor Amy, who was driving, spoke much on the way to Banklyn, and preferred Petroc Trelawney's choice of music on the Radio 3 Breakfast programme. Alex's thoughts returned again and again to Tom Kieran and Teddy Armstrong, and even more to Angus Smallwood. He had known all three, and now all three were dead.

Alex guided Amy into the car park and in an unmarked car Alex could see three men who were looking towards them. He gestured, and it was returned.

'I don't imagine this will take long, Amy.'

'Take as long as you need. I have acquired a habit I picked up from you.'

'Oh?'

'I now always carry a book with me.'

'That's good as long as it's not one of mine.'

'I did try your *Elements of Modern Philosophy*, but I gave up after reading the Foreword!'

'I should have stopped writing it at that point too though as is the way of things, the Foreword was written last.'

The three men were now waiting for him.

'Are you sure you're an ex-bishop? said the man clearly in charge, 'you don't look anywhere near old enough, and you've even brought your wife and maybe a picnic to make a day of it.'

'It's far worse than that. The lady in the car is actually my mother-in-law and she's my minder!'

There was a stunned silence.

'Well, I'm Bob Moorman, we spoke on the phone.'

'I'm Alex Elliot, Liaison Officer for the Parole Board at HMP Banklyn.'

'You understand why you are here and what you have agreed to do?'

'Yes.'

'Ok. Let's go.

They walked towards the main doors which began to open as they drew near and there was Myles waiting for them.

'Good morning Dr Elliot, officers, I'm the acting-governor, Myles Hammond. Welcome to Banklyn. I'm afraid you have to go through our security procedure. You Dr Elliot will receive your keys as usual afterwards. One of the detectives was definitely not a dog man and stood frozen to the spot as the spaniel sniffed him. Myles now led them up the iron staircase and at the top gave Alex the distinction of unlocking the gate. Then they passed through another gate and entered the governor's office where they sat down, and where, a little while later, coffee was brought for them.

'The full weekday morning staff are on duty now,' said Myles, 'No one has reported sick. People know who Dr Elliot is, and you three are with him to review the circumstances of the Parole given to Armstrong in the light of his death yesterday.'

'Thank you,' said Bob, 'and have you thought how we should proceed?'

'Yes. I will take the Liaison Officer on an inspection of the wings and the mess. When we identify your man we'll come for you.'

They set off, Alex constantly looking about him.

'Will you get the job full-time?' Alex asked Myles.

'No. I'm being moved to Durham next week. The new governor and her assistant will begin on Monday, and I leave on Wednesday. I've been told that I failed to see what was going on. Rough justice!'

'Her?'

'Yes, the new boss is a woman, as they have already at Belmarsh.'

They went through the wings but Alex couldn't identify anyone as the officer he had seen handling the drugs. Myles now led him into the staff mess where a number of officers were sitting with their drinks in their coffee break. Then the daftest thing imaginable happened. An officer seeing Alex waved a greeting which Alex returned.

'That's the man,' said Alex to Myles.

'Mr Pickles.'

'I'll go and speak with him whilst you go and bring the detectives.'

'Ok,' said Myles, and they shook hands before Myles left. Alex wandered over to the table where Pickles sat.

'It's always nice to see you Dr Elliot, but what are you doing here?'

'I have to make a report to the Parole Board in the light of what happened yesterday in Leeds and before the new governor arrives.'

'Oh yes, a terrible business, but there won't be many tears shed for Teddy. He was a horrible man and had done terrible things to children.'

At that moment Myles returned with three men, one of whom walked towards the table where Alex and Pickles were sitting. With the minimum of fuss Pickles was asked to accompany the other two men who led him out of the prison where he received an official caution before bing handcuffed and placed in the back of the police car.

In the meantime Bob had asked Myles to open Pickles's locker where they found a quantity of spice and weed, intended no doubt for his own use. Bob brought out an evidence bag and put it in.

'Thank you Dr Elliot. You may have to give evidence in court but we'll let you know. If he's sensible he'll plead guilty and he might just get lucky.'

They shook hands and Bob departed. Two of the prison officers present came up to to Alex. 'No great loss, sir,' said one of them, 'and at least the air quality should improve!'

Poor Angus Smallwood. He had been made the fall guy for what probably everyone knew, that thanks to Kelly, at least the line of command including the person who had done the final deed, had been arrested. Alex shook hands with Myles and wished him well in Durham, handed back his keys and took his leave, the big doors electronically closing behind him. The police had already left and he could see Amy engrossed in her book.

'I've only ever seen an arrest like that on television,' she said. 'It was most exciting.'

'He was called Mr Pickles. The name rings a bell but I can't think what it is.'

'Wilfred Pickles! A Yorkshireman who was very big on the wireless in the 1950s. He had various catchphrases, such as "Give him the money, Mabel", the lady in question being his wife. He was the first-ever newsreader on the BBC with a regional accent, introduced in the hope of stopping Nazi impersonation of news readers using received pronunciation.'

'Amy, you are not old enough to remember any of that.'

'Of course not, but it's part of the English tradition that has been passed down the ages even if it never quite reached you.'

'Well it's a tradition that I suspect will be of little comfort to Mr Pickles now on his way to a police cell in Hull. And as far as I'm concerned it's good riddance to him and it's good riddance to Banklyn. I shan't be returning and I shall resign as their Liaison Officer in the next couple of days. It's brought me a great deal of discomfort and I can well do without that.'

'I'm sure that's the right decision, Alex. It's an unpleasant world and I'm sure it must make those who work in it very cynical indeed. You don't need that but you never know what's coming next.'

'In fact I may do. Although she hasn't said anything to me about it yet, though she may have done so to you, I saw a used pregnancy testing kit in Emily's open handbag this morning and there was definitely a blue line. Although I love the twins totally, if she is indeed pregnant I would be over the moon and hope for a single this time.'

'Honestly, I didn't know, and I expect she was waiting for a time when the two of you were no longer running a hotel for Customs and Excise and young priests who seek to run away from the parish. But, gosh, that would be wonderful but don't forget that the wife of Roger Federer had twins twice-over!'

'Thanks for your cheerful message, Amy. Whatever follows, full-time fatherhood is going to keep me busy for quite some time to come. From the very beginning I have always been determined to ensure that Emily can continue to write, and I have no intention of going back on that. I know you think I still don't have a proper spiritual foundation for my life, but my life with Em, Chloe, George and you is my spiritual foundation and if I feel I need topping up from the Christian tradition or whatever, then mostly I know where I can find it, and I can't tell you what it means for me that Nicky has asked Emily to do the John Donne book.'

Kelly and Peter were sitting in Emily's study and having returned from dropping the children off with Fiona, Emily was making cups of coffee for them. Neither were looking forward to the return to Bristol, and then for Peter the onward journey back to his parish in Cornwall. He had already decided that he would inform his vicar that he would be leaving as soon as possible though he didn't think his boss would be altogether surprised, nor stand in his way. The drive however would be a bore.

'I notice you have a number of books on John Donne on your desk,' said Kelly. 'Are you doing something special on him?'

'Yes, my publisher has commissioned a new series by poets on poets, and although I'm quite convinced she would do a better job of it, she has insisted that I do it, and I can't believe my good luck. The circumstance of his life is almost as astonishing as his poetry, and what he says about love has rarely been matched. Others have written love poems and some are very good and I include in that WH Auden or Elizabeth Barrett Browning, but for sheer consistency none can match John Donne.

'I should of course be extremely glad to spend the whole morning with you discussing and introducing his poetry to you, but I'm not at all sure that's what you want to speak about.'

'Emily,' said Kelly, 'Peter and I have quite a past between us. As you will know, not on the basis of any malice at all, Peter found himself being assumed to be gay because he spent all his time with friends who were, not least because in the stuffy Church of England at least the Anglo-Catholics exhibited colour and fun and laughter. When he left theological college and came to the diocese, he went to see the Bishop of Truro, also known as your husband, to tell him what he thought was the truth, that he was gay because he must be gay because all those he thought he knew well told him he was. When he tried it out for size, it didn't fit, and he also began wondering if that was not also the same with regard to being a priest. Then one day, the world fell in, and he met a 6'1" lady with short blonde hair and very slim, overlooking the sea.'

'This lady I met,' said Peter taking over, 'I fell in love with immediately and in a couple of days went up to see her in Bristol and have been seeing her ever since. As you know she is a technological genius, and even to call her a genius is probably to understate. Unlike me, she has a history of relationships with men and admits she easily gets bored which is why she has chosen a profession that makes great demands upon her brain. She is not religious at all so the idea of shacking up with a priest goes against the grain, but she tells me again and again that what we have been discovering together is quite different from anything she has known before and in her own inimitable fashion she says it's akin to the difference between an Amstrad and a top of the range Mac (which I gather she made you buy). Now if I say I want to marry her and want to live the rest of my life with her, I hope you will understand that it is simply so that I can get my computer mended when everything goes wrong. The other reason is that I simply adore her and want to be there for her, and when we are both ready, to have children of our own as glorious as yours.'

'Being made for each other,' said Emily, 'means recognising that we don't have to be identical in every way, that we can even have different ways of understanding the nature of what it is to be us. The possibility that Alex and I could ever have got together would hardly have been countenanced by the most optimistic bookmaker. To this day we are both independent in terms of how we think, though not quite as much as we were when we first met, but this doesn't in any way detract from the wonder of the love we have for one another. I can't see that being any different for you. Have you decided where you want to make your base, Kelly?'

'Because I'm going to be less involved on a day-to-day basis with operations, we could quite easily go anywhere, even to Scotland. I've never given serious thought to London but, after talking it through with Peter, I think the answer is that we should remain in Bristol. As a city we love it.'

'And what would you be looking to do, Peter?'

'I mentioned to Alex that there's a job I'd like to apply for, working women straight out of prison.'

'That sounds challenging, to say the least, but Kelly, do tell me, has anyone proposed marriage to you recently?'

'Alas, no.'

'Well, tell him from me to get on with it! I highly recommend it.'

'Thank you Em, thank you so much.'

Peter and Kelly set off before Amy and Alex had returned. Emily had in the meantime gone to collect the children and over lunch they all told their stories of the morning. Alex was so relieved to know that things were working out for Peter but also for Kelly. To have Peter waiting for her at home would make such a difference, though he thought the idea that she would be less involved in operations a case of wishful thinking. He knew she wouldn't be able to resist. He was also quite bowled over by the fact that they had chosen not to talk to him about these things but to Emily, recognising in her the wisdom he knew and which those who read her poetry already knew.

His own account of the morning was straightforward, and he said he was glad to have reached the end with Banklyn, though there was one final matter he had to deal with. After lunch, the twins had a sleep, and it gave Alex the chance to make a phone call to Mrs Gathercole in Penrith.

'Ah, Dr Elliot, I did wonder if I might hear from you.'

'It's against the rules, but I felt I needed to speak to you. What has happened has come as quite a shock to me, but must have been even more so to you. I imagine that when you had heard Armstrong had been given parole you would have been shocked.'

'No, not at all. The thing is Dr Elliot we, that is Tom and me, deliberately misled you when you came to see us. We had agreed that before you came to see us. Although we had split up and divorced mainly because of Tom's drinking, I never of course stopped loving him and sometimes we would meet in Keswick. More than anything else he wanted revenge, he wanted Armstrong dead and he told me one day that he had bought a gun from the huntsman of the Blencathra Foxhounds. We both knew there was nothing possible until Armstrong applied for parole. We went through the motions of opposing it in the hearing of our friends, and in what we said to you, but on the day the Board met and we made our submissions, we both said that enough was enough and that we thought Teddy should now be given the opportunity to live again as a free man. I could tell that the chairwoman was taken aback by this, and I added that I thought that no matter how awful his crime, it was now a very long time ago and that he should be given a second chance. Tom said the same.'

'But he was to be given a new name and identity and would be living where no one knew.'

'Tom's cousin's lass works at the Home Office. Over the years she's been very useful in providing information about Armstrong. Although the justice ministry split away from the Home Office, they're still on the same computer network. She told us the result of the Board that evening and would have told us his alias and address had it not been for whoever it was came to Tom and provided him with it. If anyone knew what she'd done, I suspect she would be for the high jump, so I beg you not to say anything, because in the end it wasn't her who provided Tom with the most important information he needed which was the address in Leeds.

'Tom had said for many years that he died with the girls, so it didn't surprise me that having meted out justice to Armstrong, he should take his own life.'

Alex sat down on the sofa. He felt quite assaulted, battered and bruised by lies and deceit, and he considered how easily they had led to murder and treachery.

Seeing him looking not just reflective but rather darker than that, Emily came and sat next to him, taking his hand in hers.

'Mum tells me you've seen a blue line where you shouldn't have been looking in the first place. Well, my darling, you're quite right – another Elliot is coming, and I hope that is more than capable of lightening your load.'

'Em, that's so wonderful. How clever you are.'

He released his hand and took hold of her instead.

'I do seem to remember that you were there too.'

'So I was, but to remind me we could have an afternoon rest

upstairs now.'

A little voice sounding upstairs told them they might have to wait.

'I'll go,' said Alex.

'Ok, and while you're there I'll make an appointment for you.'

'Appointment? What for?'

'The opticians of course.'

'Oh!'

Printed in Great Britain
by Amazon